Sound! Euphonium

Welcome to the Kitauji High School Concert Band

Ayano Takeda

YEN ON
New York

Sound! Euphonium
Ayano Takeda

Translation by Paul Starr
Cover art by Nikki Asada

'HIBIKE! EUPHONIUM -KITAUJI KOKO SUISOGAKUBU E YOKOSO-' by Ayano Takeda
Copyright © 2013 Ayano Takeda
All rights reserved.
Original Japanese edition published by Takarajimasha, Inc., Tokyo.
English translation rights arranged with Takarajimasha, Inc. through Tuttle-Mori Agency, Inc., Tokyo

English translation © 2017 by Yen Press, LLC

Yen On
1290 Avenue of the Americas
New York, NY 10104

Visit us at yenpress.com
facebook.com/yenpress
twitter.com/yenpress
yenpress.tumblr.com
instagram.com/yenpress

First Yen On Edition: June 2017

Yen On is an imprint of Yen Press, LLC.
The Yen On name and logo are trademarks of Yen Press, LLC.

Library of Congress Cataloging-in-Publication Data
Names: Takeda, Ayano, author. | Starr, Paul Tuttle, translator. | Asada, Nikki, artist.
Title: Sound! euphonium : welcome to the Kitauji High School Concert Band / Ayano Takeda ;
translation by Paul Starr ; cover art by Nikki Asada.
Description: First Yen On edition. | New York, NY : Yen On, 2017–
Identifiers: LCCN 2017002261 | ISBN 9780316558594 (paperback)
Subjects: | CYAC: Bands (Music)—Fiction. | High schools—Fiction. | Schools—Fiction. |
Friendship—Fiction.
Classification: LCC PZ7.1.T34 So 2017 | DDC [Fic]—dc23
LC record available at https://lccn.loc.gov/2017002261

ISBNs: 978-0-316-55859-4 (paperback)
978-0-316-55980-5 (ebook)

1 3 5 7 9 10 8 6 4 2

LSC-C

Printed in the United States of America

♫ Contents ♪

Prologue   1

1   Nice to Meet You, Euphonium   5

2   I'm Home, Festival   37

3   Welcome Back, Audition   87

4   Good-Bye, Competition   135

Epilogue   185

♪ Prologue ♪

Hundreds of gazes focused on the same spot. The atmosphere was tinged with a swirling, feverish energy that brought a flush to the girls' faces. Kumiko slowly exhaled, trying to steel herself against the contagious emotion. Her heartbeat hammered in her eardrums. Her fingernails pressed crescent-shaped marks into the sweat-sticky palms of her clenched fists.

"I'm so nervous I might actually die," murmured Azusa next to her, unable to endure the tension silently.

"Me too," replied Kumiko, her rapt eyes widening.

ALL-KYOTO CONCERT BAND COMPETITION, read the simple, vertically lettered sign. In pursuit of making it to the Kansai Regionals, this was the third time Kumiko had come to this concert hall since starting middle school. She unconsciously tightened her fists.

"This is it—" came the words from no one in particular. Men carrying a large sheet of paper slowly advanced to the front of the stage. All eyes were upon them. Kumiko felt like her heart was going to leap, flea-like, out of her chest. She was feverish and faint. She pressed her hands hard against her reddening cheeks and watched the paper intently.

The men slowly unrolled the banner, revealing a list of middle schools. Next to the names were written the characters for "gold," "silver," and "bronze." Before Kumiko could even think of finding her school, Azusa's voice rose in a delighted shout.

"Gold!"

The exclamation spread infectiously and was soon followed by shrill cries. "Gold! We did it!"

Some schools were shouting in celebration, but others had fallen silent at the stark reality of the results displayed before them. Kumiko noticed that the students from another school next to them looked like they were at a funeral. She hesitated briefly, unable to be as happy as she imagined she was supposed to be.

"Kumiko! What're you spacing out for? We got gold! Gold!"

Feeling Azusa's sudden embrace, Kumiko finally let a smile slip. "...Yeah. Thank goodness."

"I'm gonna go tell Asami. She was so nervous she shut herself up in the bathroom."

"Gotcha. Just don't be late for the closing."

"Roger that!" replied Azusa cheerfully before heading farther into the hall. Her black hair was tied back into a ponytail that bobbed as she went.

Kumiko slowly opened her locked fists and looked out again at the banner displaying the results. "Gold Prize" was indeed written next to her middle school's name.

It was gold, all right, but fool's gold—they wouldn't be advancing to the All-Kansai regional competition. Still, it felt like a passing grade. She glanced at their director, who wore a satisfied expression and was heartily applauding. *Thank goodness! We got gold!* Within Kumiko, the reality of it was slowly beginning to sink in. She breathed a sigh of relief, and with it, her legs untensed. She realized anew just how nerve-racked she'd been.

Kumiko was just about to congratulate the others in her instrument section when she sensed something was off. Her gaze wandered as she searched for its source, and then quite suddenly, her gaze met Reina's. She was standing there stock-still and unsmiling, her trumpet gripped tightly in her hands.

"Are you crying from happiness?"

At Kumiko's timid question, Reina silently shook her head. Her eyes radiated her intensity, but a skim of moisture was welling up in them.

"...ate this."

"Huh?"

"I hate it. I hate it so much I could die. Why is everybody so happy about gold? I thought we were aiming for Nationals."

Tears began spilling from Reina's eyes. Kumiko hastily broke her gaze, as if to escape. Her own face suddenly burned with heat. She was ashamed of having been so relieved to get gold. "...Did you seriously think we could've made it to Nationals?"

Reina violently wiped her eyes, then sniffed. Her pale pink lips quivered in accusation and anger. "You mean you *don't* hate it?" she spat, and her accusation stabbed right through Kumiko's heart. "Well, I do. I really, really hate this."

Her strained voice carved itself with unpleasant clarity into Kumiko's brain.

It was the last competition of middle school.

When she remembered the moment, it was always Reina's eyes that came to mind. And whenever she thought of them, Kumiko wanted to run as far away from that summer as she could.

1 ♪ Nice to Meet You, Euphonium ♪

Dark blue skirts fell just above the knee. Below them, in neat rows in the school gymnasium, were pairs of pale legs. Skinny legs, thick legs. The boys fidgeted in their stiff collars as they stole furtive glances. The girls seemed not to notice as they openly displayed their youthful skin. Kumiko took in all of this absentmindedly, then looked down to regard her own form: a girl of meager physique wearing a dark blue sailor-style school uniform. She wondered why she'd believed the rumor that your chest got bigger when you started high school. She sneaked a peek at the girl next to her, whose generous curves were evident even under the uniform's material, and sighed.

Kitauji Prefectural High School was famous for its cute sailor suit uniforms—they were the only sailor-style uniforms in Uji city and well regarded even by students from other schools in the region. Academically, Kitauji was on the better end of the middle range, but its college admissions record was nothing to write home about. Kumiko had chosen Kitauji because of the uniform. If she was going to end up at a school more or less like this one anyway, then she preferred the one with the cute uniform. Yet despite the superficial criterion she'd used to make her decision, now that she was finally wearing the uniform, she strangely didn't feel particularly cute. Kumiko had recently been preoccupied with a wish to have been born beautiful.

"Continuing with our program, please stand for the singing of the school song."

At the vice-principal's words, everyone moved. Kumiko stood, too, not wanting to seem sluggish to react. On the stage was displayed a large sheet containing the school song's lyrics for the benefit of the new students. In middle school there hadn't been many students who actually sang the school song, but Kumiko didn't know whether that would carry over to high school. She looked carefully around her to avoid being the odd one out. The rest of the entering student body looked just as uncertain. Maybe they were doing the same thing she was.

On the stage, the concert band readied their instruments, with serious expressions on their faces. A girl with a scary-looking expression on her face readied a conductor's baton. The golden euphoniums glittered beneath the fluorescent lights. As Kumiko watched, her breath momentarily caught in her throat. The conductor raised her hand, and the next instant, all the instruments raised their various faces. The trumpet section seemed to aim directly at Kumiko. She was certain she heard the sound of the whole band taking a breath. The baton flicked sharply up, then came slicing down.

"...Oh, this is bad," said Kumiko in spite of herself. The sounds assaulting her ears were horribly dissonant. The rhythm was off, and the tempo was all over the place. The sounds coming from the band were utterly unrelated to the baton's movements. She'd planned to continue in concert band in high school, but if this was the best they could do, she would pass. Forget about the Kansai Regionals—even the All-Kyoto Competition was off the table for this group.

Unconcerned with Kumiko's rumination, the band played on. She could hear the teachers singing from where they stood by the gym's walls, but it didn't seem like a single student was joining in. The performance finally ended, and the students took their seats. The entrance ceremony continued, but Kumiko's mind was filled with uncertainty and anticipation regarding what might await her in high school. Which club would she join? Would she be able to make any friends? What would her homeroom teacher be like?

"Moving on, we'll now have a word from a representative for the entering students, Reina Kousaka."

At the sound of the familiar name, Kumiko looked up with a sharp breath. "Here!" The clear voice echoed across the gymnasium as a sailor-suited beauty stood. She had long, shiny black hair and large, expressive eyes. Her back was ramrod straight, and she radiated confidence.

Reina Kousaka.

She had attended the same middle school as Kumiko and had played in the same concert band. With her excellent grades and good reputation among their teachers, it wasn't remotely surprising she'd been picked as the representative for the entering class. But given Reina's brains, she definitely could've gotten into a better school than this one—so why had she decided to come here? There was no way it had anything to do with the uniform. Kumiko craned her neck to get a better view, and suddenly Reina faced her, her obsidian eyes directed right at Kumiko. *Is she looking at me?* The pair's gaze definitely met. It was only an instant, but to Kumiko it felt much longer. Reina's expression softened, and then she looked ahead as though nothing had happened. Her lips parted to speak, and the words came to her without any hesitation.

Representative for the entering students. Kumiko repeated the stately title in her mind and gave a soft sigh.

"Heya! What's your name?" came the voice, no sooner than Kumiko had taken her seat in the classroom of Year 1, Class 3. She looked over to see the grinning face of a girl with short hair. White teeth shone past slightly parted fine lips. Her noticeably tanned skin hinted at her participation in a sports club of some kind. She was not the kind of girl Kumiko had ever had much to do with. Kumiko smiled pleasantly to hide her agitation.

"I'm Kumiko Oumae."

"Kumiko, huh? I'm Hazuki Katou. You can call me Hazuki,

Katou, whatever!" said Hazuki, leaning over the desk. Even though she thought the other girl was being awfully familiar, Kumiko turned to face her.

"So where'd you go to middle school? Not Higashichu, right?"

"I went to Kitachu."

"Kitachu? Wow, don't see that too much!" Hazuki's eyes widened in surprise. "I dunno why, but Kitauji's lousy with kids from Higashichu. That's where I went, too, but now I'm seeing so many people I know it barely feels like I'm actually in high school, y'know?"

"It must be nice to have lots of friends, though. I'm envious."

"No, no, no, it's no good at all! It's the *worst* when people know you from middle school. It totally wrecks your high school debut!"

"I'm sure that's not true."

"Oh, it's true, all right. That's why I suffered through dyeing my hair. Really wished I could've done red or something, though," said Hazuki, twirling her hair around her finger. It seemed excessive for a "high school debut" to Kumiko, but she kept herself from saying so.

"But anyway, I was wondering—how come you use standard Japanese?"

"Hmm. Because I used to live in Tokyo, I guess?"

"Huh! You didn't pick up Kansai dialect?"

"My whole family just uses standard Japanese, so I never really picked up Kansai dialect. Oh, but my friends complain about the opposite—like, 'I'm catching standard from you!'"

"Hmm. I'll have to make sure it doesn't rub off on me, then," said Hazuki nonchalantly, resting her chin in her hand. Her right cheek was smushed upward so that it seemed like she was vaguely smiling.

Kumiko was about to ask her why, but then with terrible timing, the teacher entered the classroom. She looked to be in her early fifties, her white hair tied back. There was something imposing about her. She considered the assembled class with a sharp glance, then cleared her throat loudly.

"Take your seats."

The voice was quiet but somehow commanding, and the classroom went instantly from noise to silence. The students who had just been chattering quickly found their seats, which were arranged in alphabetical order. "Whoa, scary," murmured Hazuki.

"I can't say that I'm particularly impressed with the noisy classroom, given that you're all high school students. A high school education is not compulsory, a fact of which you should all be quite aware."

The formerly feverish atmosphere of the room instantly chilled. The teacher breathed a resigned sigh, then picked up a piece of chalk with one bony hand, putting white characters on the green blackboard's surface.

"I am Michie Matsumoto, the homeroom teacher for Year 1, Class 3. I teach music, and I'm the assistant director for the concert band."

At the words "concert band," Hazuki visibly perked up.

"You should all know that I pride myself on being the strictest teacher in the school. Understand that I have no intention of coddling you," declared Michie as she deliberately took out a black portfolio. "I'll now take attendance. When your name is called, answer clearly. Asai, Yuudai."

"Here!"

"Ishikawa, Yuki."

"Here!"

During attendance in middle school, students got by with a lazily raised hand. Evidently in high school, a proper response was required. Kumiko wondered if rules just generally got stricter as adulthood approached, or if this teacher was just scary.

"—Oumae, Kumiko."

"...Uh, here!" In her thoughtful reverie, Kumiko had stopped listening, and her hasty response broke the tense atmosphere of the classroom. Hazuki grinned over at her. Kumiko couldn't help but look down at her desk out of embarrassment.

"—Katou, Hazuki."

"Here!"

"Kawashima... Ryokuki?" For the first time, a puzzled look came over Michie's face. Right in front of the teacher, the fluffy-haired girl whose name had interrupted roll call tentatively raised her hand.

"S-sorry. It's pronounced 'Sapphire.' The characters are 'green' and 'shine,' but they're pronounced 'Sapphire.'"

Sapphire? The murmured word rippled through the classroom. The girl seemed terribly embarrassed by her own name, her already petite form withering as she shrank further and further into her seat.

"Excuse me—Sapphire, then. I'll be sure to get it right in the future," said Michie before briskly moving on to the next name. The murmuring class, too, fell immediately quiet again. But still—"Sapphire"? The girl had better be pretty with a name like that, Kumiko mused, looking ahead at her. Unfortunately, as Kumiko was seated well back in the classroom, she couldn't see the girl's face.

"Sapphire, huh? What a cool name!" whispered Hazuki.

Hazuki's aesthetic sense certainly was peculiar, thought Kumiko.

"That will be all for today. Make sure you all apply yourselves in tomorrow's academic placement tests."

With those words from the homeroom teacher, the first day of high school came to a close. Kumiko sighed with worry—she hadn't done any studying at all since finishing her high school entrance examinations.

"Hey, Kumiko, where d'you live? Let's go home together."

Kumiko was still packing her textbooks into her schoolbag, but Hazuki was standing right in front of her, totally ready to go. From her black leather backpack hung a keychain with a trumpet charm on it.

"I live near Byoudou-in. Is that the right direction for you?" said Kumiko.

"Sure is. I take the Keihan line to Oubaku Station."

"Oh, really? We live close to each other, then," replied Kumiko, standing. There was nothing decorative attached to her bag. She didn't much care for that kind of clutter. "Hazuki, did you do concert band in middle school? I saw your trumpet charm," she said, pointing to the keychain.

Hazuki laughed energetically. "Nope! I was super into tennis club."

"You do seem like the athletic type."

"'Cause of my tan, right? You get it practicing. I used to be a lot paler." Hazuki grinned, rolling up her sleeves as proof. Her tan was starting to fade in places, becoming more of a patchy, school-uniform tan. "Oh, but I'm planning on doing band in high school. Seems fun!"

"Oh, really? I did band in middle school."

"For real? Are you gonna keep it up here?"

Kumiko was about to answer that she hadn't decided yet, but just as she was opening her mouth to speak, a third party cut her off.

"Um, are you two planning on joining the concert band?"

Hazuki and Kumiko looked up at the source of the voice. Standing there was the fluffy-haired girl from earlier—the one with the absolutely unforgettable name. Sapphire Kawashima. The peculiarly named girl had a gentle, almost meek appearance.

"Oh, Sapphire!" Hazuki called her by name without a trace of derision, but when the girl heard it, her face turned as red as a lobster.

"Um, I'm sorry, but would you please not call me that?"

"Huh? Why?"

"I just really hate my name. It's so humiliating."

"It's so cool, though! 'Sapphire'! I love it!"

"Some people might think it's cool, but hardly anybody can read the characters, and it's just really embarrassing," said Sapphire, looking downcast. Inwardly, Kumiko agreed entirely with the girl. If Kumiko'd been given a name like that, she was certain it'd constantly overshadow her.

"So please, call me Midori."

"Midori! Okay! You got it." Hazuki nodded, slapping Sapphire's back heartily. That might have been Hazuki's idea of friendly physical contact, but Sapphire's—*Midori's*—delicate frame wobbled unsteadily at the sudden violence. "So where'd you go to middle school, Midori? Let's walk home together!"

Midori looked questioningly to Kumiko, as if asking permission. Kumiko smiled and gave an enthusiastic nod. *Of course!*

Outside the school's front entrance, the air was faintly chilly. The courtyard was enclosed by a border of sakura cherry trees, which were already shedding their pink petals, and pale green buds were hesitantly beginning to peek out from the slender branches. The students passing beneath seemed uninterested in the scattering blossoms; not a single one paid them any mind. To Kumiko, the students in their matching uniforms all seemed to wear the same expression.

"Um, I went to Seijo. I did private school for elementary and middle school, so."

"Wait, but Seijo's got an incredible concert band," said Kumiko.

Hazuki made a surprised face. "Oh yeah?"

"Yeah, they're amazing. They make it to Nationals all the time."

"Whoa! That *is* something."

Hearing this, Midori bashfully rubbed the back of her head. When the sun shone through her fluffy hair, it turned a golden brown. "Um, I'm nothing special, but our director was amazing."

"Does the director have much to do in band? It always looks like they just kinda…play."

"They definitely don't 'just play.' Just like how a team captain has a big effect on a sports club, a great adviser can make a band a lot better," explained Kumiko.

"Huh, how 'bout that." Hazuki nodded, seemingly impressed. She sent a pebble skittering off with a kick from the sole of her shoe. The walk was smoothly paved with a thick smear of asphalt, and there wasn't a single weed to be seen. "What instrument did you play, Midori?"

"I play contrabass and have for ages!"

"Contrabass? The heck's that?"

Midori pouted at Hazuki's question. "It's like a big old violin! It's super-supercool!"

"O-oh, yeah?" said Hazuki with a nod, taken aback by Midori's sudden intensity.

"Contrabass, huh," murmured Kumiko, watching the exchange

out of the corner of her eye. Midori looked to be 150 centimeters tall—at least ten centimeters shorter than Kumiko. Kumiko had a hard time imagining someone Midori's size playing an instrument nearly two meters tall.

"What about you, Kumiko?" asked Midori.

"Huh?"

"What instrument did you play? You said you did concert band in middle school, right?"

While Kumiko had been distracted by her own thoughts, Midori had come alongside her and was now peering curiously at her face in a way Kumiko couldn't help but associate with an adorable little animal of some kind. "I played eupho."

"Wow! Eupho!"

"Whaddaya mean, a UFO?"

While Midori's eyes sparkled at Kumiko's answer, Hazuki's face turned dubious. She'd probably never heard the term used to refer to an instrument before. It was a reaction Kumiko was well accustomed to.

"Not a 'UFO,' a *eupho*. A euphonium. It's in the bass section... It's a relatively minor instrument, though."

"Huh! I'd definitely want to play something flashy. Like trumpet, or sax!"

"Yeah, that happens kinda a lot. Most of the bass instruments are pretty plain. When I first started band, even I was thinking I wanted to play the flute," said Midori with a chagrined smile. True, she definitely seemed more the flute type.

"Are you going to do concert band in high school, too, Midori?"

"Yeah, for sure!"

Kumiko was taken aback by the speedy answer, but Hazuki's eyes sparkled. "Really? Then we're gonna be in the same club!"

"Still... Our school's club is... well, kinda..."

As Kumiko fumbled for words, Midori finished the thought like she'd read Kumiko's mind. "They're so bad."

"Oh yeah? They sounded pretty normal to me," said Hazuki, tilting her head.

Over the years, the skill of high school concert bands had steadily risen. The same performance would have sounded very different to someone with ensemble experience, like Kumiko, than it did to the inexperienced Hazuki.

Midori laughed at Hazuki's response. "They probably couldn't even get a silver medal at the city competition with that performance. No way they'd have any chance at fool's gold and forget about going to Kansai."

"What's 'fool's gold'?"

"Schools that move on to the Kansai Regionals are chosen from the ones that win a gold prize. But when you win gold and still don't progress, that's called fool's gold."

Just hearing the words "fool's gold" was enough to dampen Kumiko's mood. "Midori, you said you went to Seijo? Can you deal with a band as bad as Kitauji's?" she asked, trying to change the subject.

The girl scratched her cheek as she thought it over, then answered in a thoughtful voice. "As long as I get to play my instrument, I'm happy, so I'm not too worried about the level. Just so long as it's fun."

"Oh."

"What about you, Kumiko?"

"Huh?" When Kumiko was asked the obvious question, her voice caught. She hadn't decided which club she was going to join, but she was hesitant to even admit that much. A strange silence briefly fell over the trio.

Hazuki threw her arm over Kumiko's shoulder as if to dispel the awkward moment. "You're gonna join band, right, Kumiko?" she asked innocently. Who could refuse that face?

Kumiko managed an awkward smile and nodded like she was conceding defeat. "Y-yeah...I plan to."

Evidently pleased with the answer, Midori beamed. "Oh, good! I was super worried about whether I'd be able to make friends in the band."

"Guess the three of us better get along!" said Hazuki energetically. Seeing the two other girls smile, Kumiko started to feel like her own decision hadn't been wrong at all. But even as she mused that maybe it wasn't such a bad thing to go with the flow, she remembered the concert band's performance at the entrance ceremony and quietly sighed.

Not far from the exit at Keihan line's Uji station was a bridge—Uji Bridge. If you went for a walk there in the early morning, you could see the vermilion red bridges spanning the water to an island called Tounoshima and drink in the spot's scenic beauty that could have been a tourist attraction. Then if you made the crossing and turned left, you'd end up on Byoudou-in Avenue.

The street was lined with historic teashops and traditional sweet shops, and it was Kumiko's very favorite place. The scent of tea that drifted on the breeze was enough to fill her heart to the brim. As she walked down the cobblestone way, the entrance to Byoudou-in temple came into view—but since entering the grounds proper took an admission fee, the main shrine remained out of sight.

"So you're going to Kitauji, huh?"

The shock from hearing those words interrupted Kumiko's pleasant walk. It was like someone had shoved her from behind. She lurched forward, then quickly recovered and looked over her shoulder. "What's your problem?"

"Just happened to see you, is all."

The answer and the feigned innocence belonged to Kumiko's old childhood friend, Shuuichi Tsukamoto. He was slim-framed and about 170 centimeters tall. He'd been in the same middle school concert band as Kumiko and through some twist of fate had also been in her homeroom class for three years running. Their high school, however, divided homerooms into science and humanities tracks, which had finally kept them out of the same class.

"You never told me you were going to Kitauji."

"So what?"

"It would've been the normal thing to do. We did wind up at the same school, after all."

"Hmm. Normal, huh." Kumiko curled one corner of her mouth

up meaningfully, then turned on her heel away from Shuuichi. The Ajirogi Path that led away from Byoudou-in Avenue ran alongside Uji River, and Kumiko could take it all the way home to her family's apartment.

"Hey, wait up," said Shuuichi hastily, lengthening his stride and drawing alongside Kumiko. They lived in the same apartment building. "What're you so mad about?"

"What am I so mad about? Are you seriously asking that?" shot back Kumiko without so much as looking at Shuuichi.

He folded his arms and *hmm*ed, seeming to give the question some thought. "There aren't really any clues."

"Is that so. Well, good-bye," said Kumiko, turning to leave Shuuichi behind right then and there, but he hastily grabbed her arm.

"Wait, wait, wait! Don't just ignore me!"

"In that case, I would like an apology for what you said."

"Ugh, what's with that cold formality?"

"I am being neither cold nor formal."

"Liar," said Shuuichi with a defeated sigh. In his black uniform with its stiff, high collar, he looked taller and rangier than he had in middle school. He had been shorter than Kumiko, once upon a time. Irritated at now having to look up at him in order to properly see his face, Kumiko smacked him on the back, and he rewarded her with a fake-sounding "Ouch!"

"Back in the last year of middle school, you said, 'I got nothin' to say to you, ugly!'"

"Oh, uh, that was…y'know…" Shuuichi was obviously flustered. Perhaps he'd finally remembered his own words.

"That was what?"

"I mean, you just asked me if you could come over for dinner that night, in front of a bunch of other guys. Right in the middle of puberty like that—I was trying to hide how embarrassed I was."

"What kind of excuse is that? Are you saying it would've bothered you if somebody knew we were eating dinner together?"

"No, not *bothered*, just, like…it was kind of embarrassing."

"Oh okay then I see how it is that's fine please stay away from me."

"Spare me the run-on sentences! It's been, what, a year? Would you just forgive me already? Plus, my mom misses you. She keeps asking when you're coming over again."

"If you apologize, I might consider it."

"Fine, fine. I'm sorry, I'm sorry!"

"My god, that's even worse," said Kumiko, furrowing her brows and not even trying to hide her anger.

Shuuichi pressed his palms together and repeated, "I'm sorry, I'm sorry."

There was something comical about a big guy hunching over in apology like that, and Kumiko finally capitulated with a sigh. "Fine, whatever. Who even cares."

"Ah! So you forgive me, then!"

"I didn't really say anything about forgiving you, but."

"Aah, I understand. My apologies."

Kumiko glanced at the self-satisfied boy next to her and sniffed. She shifted her bag full of textbooks to her left shoulder, slowed her brisk walk, and shrugged faintly. "...So which club do you plan on joining?"

Perhaps Shuuichi was relieved at the change of subject as his expression softened visibly. The unfashionable sneakers his mother had probably bought for him made a small sound as he kicked at the path's pavement stones. "Yeah, I'm still thinking about that."

"You're just going to do band again, aren't you?"

"C'mon, what's with the 'just'? What're *you* gonna do?"

"Me? I'll...probably do band."

"Just band *again*? So you're not one to talk."

"I really hadn't planned on it, though," said Kumiko, pursing her lips.

"So why do it?" said Shuuichi, peering at her. Kumiko looked away, trying on a noncommittal smile as a smoke screen. But her old friend seemed to see right through it. "Or was it that thing you do—just going with the flow?"

"...Mm, something like that."

"Don't you think it's time to fix that already? You gotta be able to speak your mind, or it's trouble."

"I know." Kumiko became quiet at the pseudo-lecture. It wasn't very funny, somehow.

"Still, if you're gonna join, I might as well. Wonder what instrument I should do..." said Shuuichi lightly, stretching. The pale insides of his wrists peeked out from under his cuffs. It seemed to Kumiko that there was something catlike about him.

"Is that really how you should choose which club to join?"

"Sure, why not? I'm lousy at sports, so it's not like I have much of a selection to begin with."

"...Ah," Kumiko murmured, as brusquely as she could manage. Her brand-new dark brown loafers shone dully in the evening sun's light.

The boy in front of her smiled bashfully, then transparently changed the subject. "Hey, so apparently there's a superhot girl in our class." Hearing this, Kumiko kicked him in the back as hard as she could.

Club activities started in earnest near the end of April, about two weeks after the entrance ceremony. The potential new members of the concert band had gathered in the music classroom and taken their seats, expressions of uncertainty on all their faces. They were surrounded by senior band members, one of whom was the scary-looking girl who'd wielded the baton during the band's entrance ceremony performance.

"I don't think we're going to get any more than this, President," a girl holding a clarinet murmured to the scary-looking girl. Kumiko glanced furtively around. Fewer than thirty new students were seated there, and scattered among them were faces she recognized.

"Yeah? I guess this is about it, then." The girl who'd been called President stroked her chin thoughtfully. From her neck hung a large saxophone—a baritone sax. She walked to the front of the classroom and took a deep breath.

"All right, everybody. It's nice to meet you. I'm the president of the concert band, Haruka Ogasawara. I play the baritone sax, so any sax hopefuls will see a lot of me," said Ogasawara with a pleasant smile. She had the strong voice you'd expect from a club president.

"Our concert band has a lot of history, and we were a well-known name in competitions up until about ten years ago. We even went to Nationals…although we're pretty out of shape now."

The music room's walls were festooned with the honors the concert band had won, including multiple appearances at the Kansai Regionals and a gold prize at Nationals. The framed photographs were old, their faded dustiness somehow melancholy.

"So, then, uh… Yes, actually this year we have a new director. Last year our director was Ms. Rikako, but she's on maternity leave this year. We'll be getting a new director, but right now we don't know much about him. At the entrance ceremony he said his name was Mr. Taki, but it seems he'll be coming a bit late today. Also, our assistant director, Ms. Michie, is busy with parent orientations today, so she won't make it. And, as a warning to first-year students, she's really scary, so try not to get her mad at you."

Ms. Michie was also Kumiko's homeroom teacher. Apparently she was as fearsome as she seemed.

"So today what we'll be doing is assigning instruments. The senior students you see standing around the classroom are representatives for each instrument. They're going to introduce their instruments as a reference for anybody who hasn't done any music before high school. Those of you with prior experience, please make sure to inform us. Each instrument has a different affinity, so we'll be taking that and your individual aptitude into account as we assign them. No complaining if we don't assign you the one you were hoping for."

Immediately after Ogasawara finished speaking, she called the standing students over to her part of the room. The first one to step forward was a stunning girl with a trumpet. Her straight, black hair was similar to Reina's, but the impression she gave off couldn't have been more different. There was something faint and delicate about her. If Kumiko had been a male student, she mused, the girl might well have aroused her protective instincts.

The straight-haired girl bowed modestly and politely, then glanced for just a moment toward Ogasawara. Her cheeks flushed faintly, maybe from nerves. "I'm Kaori Nakaseko, the section leader for the trumpets. The trumpet is the star of the brass instruments, so I don't think I need to explain it to you. Right now we have six trumpets, and we all get along very well. We carry many of the solos and melodies, and I'm sure anyone who joins us will have a good time. We're open to students with or without experience, so please don't hesitate to apply."

Everyone applauded her introduction. Following Kaori, the instrument introductions proceeded briskly. Trombone, French horn, flute, sax, clarinet, oboe, percussion—the well-known instruments like flute or sax were popular no matter who introduced them, but competition for the more obscure parts dropped. While she'd played euphonium in middle school, Kumiko had been thinking about trying her hand at something different in high school, and her gaze wandered out the window as she mulled it over. The music room was on the third floor of the building at the campus's northernmost end, and its window offered a good view of the school's sports field. The incomprehensible shouts of the baseball and soccer clubs echoed across the grounds. Kumiko didn't get along especially well with sporty types. She could never understand what they were thinking.

"Next is the introduction to the eupho."

Hearing Ogasawara's words, Kumiko came back to herself with a sharp breath. A tall, beautiful girl with distinctive red-framed glasses came to the front of the room holding a silver euphonium. There was something about her—maybe her sharp gaze—that gave her an intellectual air. She pushed her glasses up smartly with an extended index finger, and a smile quirked at the corners of her mouth.

"I'm Asuka Tanaka, the bass section leader, and as you can see, I play the euphonium."

Some students, apparently unfamiliar with the instrument, tilted their heads at the strange term. *UFO?* Apparently anticipating this reaction, Asuka nodded heartily. "That's right! The euphonium is a piston-valved B-flat member of the tuba family. The history of the instrument is not well understood, but some believe it to be an improvement on an instrument created by the Weimar concertmaster Ferdinand Sommer called the sommerophone, but some say the modern euphonium may also have arisen as an English continuation of the Belgian Adolphe Sax's saxhorn family of instruments. It was originally known as the euphonion, which comes from the Greek *euphonos*, meaning 'of good sound.' And just as the name would suggest, the euphonium is an excellent instrument that lends a broad, mellow tone to the bass section. The history of the euphonium in Japan is uncertain, but it began in the year 1870 with the arrival of the euphonion from Britain. The military concert band was originally trained in the British style, but after the split into army and navy branches in that same year, the naval band continued in the British—and later German—style, while the army band used the French style. The parts we would now use the euphonium for went by a variety of names—in the navy bands, they were called the euphonion or the baritone horn, while the army referred to it as the petite bass or small bass. According to many of the images we have from that period, we know that the French-style bass saxhorn was used, but many ensembles, including naval and educational bands, referred to the instrument in the German way, as the baritone or euphonium, at the behest of their directors. With the proliferation of the school band introduced by the United States after the end of the Second World War, the instrument became firmly known as the euphonium, and the use of the piston valves developed in England became common. Then—"

"All right, that's enough! Asuka, you're welcome to present everything you looked up on Wikipedia, but at least try to summarize it a bit ahead of time," said the club president, cutting Asuka off despite her apparent readiness to continue for eternity. Given the mostly unchanged expressions on the faces of the other seniors, this seemed to be Asuka's standard behavior.

Asuka pouted, displaying her dissatisfaction at having been interrupted. "Aw, I haven't even gotten to talking about the eupho's many charms!"

"No, you've definitely said enough. Next! The tuba presenter, please come to the front!"

Still clearly frustrated, Asuka reluctantly retreated to her corner. The obvious question arose in Kumiko's mind: How had a person like that gotten to be section leader?

"...I'm...Takuya Gotou, on tuba."

The student who came up to replace Asuka was male and both vertically and horizontally large. In contrast to Asuka's volubility, he seemed downright gloomy. He wore glasses with thick black frames and carried an instrument that seemed like a magnified version of the euphonium that had just been explained. It was the tuba—the largest wind instrument in the ensemble.

"The tuba is a bass instrument, and it doesn't really play melodies... so it's kind of boring. Also, it weighs about ten kilos, so it's heavy. It uses something like six meters of tubing. When we march, we use a big white version called a sousaphone ... That's heavy, too..."

"..."

"..."

"Uh, is that all?" asked Ogasawara, her eyes widening in surprise.

"Um, yeah, that's all..." replied Takuya with a slightly flustered expression.

"Aw, come on, Gotou! You didn't get the tuba's appeal across at all! I suppose I, Asuka Tanaka, will have to introduce it—"

"No, you be quiet," said Ogasawara, immediately shooting down Asuka, who'd energetically raised her hand. "Normally there's one more bass part, an instrument called the contrabass. Unfortunately, since the third-year students graduated last year, we lost our contrabass section. If there are any students with any experience, please do try out. Otherwise, we're going to be in trouble."

Asuka carried the contrabass up, as if to say, *By the way, this is a contrabass!* The big stringed instrument was even taller than she was, and an impressed murmur arose from the students who hadn't known what to expect.

"Anybody played one before?" Ogasawara looked over the classroom.

In the middle of the room, a slender hand hesitantly rose. It was Midori. "Um...I played contrabass in middle school."

Asuka's eyes glittered brightly the instant they fell upon the petite girl. She pushed the instrument off on the president, then strode with purpose toward Midori. Midori's eyes went wide and she froze, overwhelmed by Asuka's presence. Asuka grabbed the girl's raised hand, her handsome profile closing in on Midori. Asuka's hair fell over her shoulder as she leaned forward and obscured her face from Kumiko's view.

"You'll do it, then?" There was something seductive in Asuka's suddenly lowered voice. Even Kumiko's heart beat a little faster.

Midori had been gazing, stunned, at the senior girl in front of her, but the words seemed to suddenly bring her back to her senses. The color of autumn leaves tinted her cheeks. "Y-yes! Um, I mean, if you're all right with just me, then I'm happy to."

"No kidding? Perfect! It's a huge help!" The seriousness from just a moment earlier vanished as Asuka flashed a big, carefree smile. *Ah, I see. This is how she psychologically manipulates people*, Kumiko quietly concluded.

"There you have it, Haruka. This one's all ours."

"Fine, fine. Whatever you say," said the president, setting the big instrument down on the floor and waving her hand dismissively. She then picked up a notebook that had been left on top of the classroom's piano. The thin notebook had *BAND MEMBER REGISTRY* written on it and appeared rather worn from heavy use.

"Okay, we're going to decide the other parts now. It'd be a pain to have each of you say what instrument you'd like to play, so instead just go over to wherever the representatives are. If you aren't chosen, then you'll move to your second choice. That's about it, so, good luck."

At Ogasawara's casually tossed-off instructions, the first-year students began to move.

"Geez, what should I do?" murmured Kumiko uncertainly as she looked in Asuka's direction. As the new contrabass, Midori seemed to have become Asuka's plaything. For some reason, Asuka was pinching Midori's cheek while an exasperated-looking Takuya looked on and tried to placate her.

"That Asuka's a trip," chuckled Hazuki, amused.

"Seems like there are a bunch of characters in the bass section."

"I mean, that's how it goes, right? Your taste in instruments says a lot about your personality."

"Does it?"

"I'm the type that wants to stick out more than supporting people, so that's why I thought the trumpet or something'd be cool." Hazuki pointed in Kaori's direction. It seemed like most of the girls gathered in the trumpet section had a certain flashiness to them. "Guess I better go line up!"

Hazuki flashed an affable smile, then inserted herself into the queue of students hoping for the trumpet. Most new students had made for the corner of the room corresponding to their preferred instrument. Kumiko was about the only one still indecisively wandering around the classroom center.

I want to play this. That one looks cool. Kumiko had no such strong preferences. She wished they'd just give her whatever instrument they had to spare. Then she wouldn't have to agonize like this. Kumiko gazed down at the palm of her hand as though searching for a destination. The fine lines crossing her palm were like a map of some nameless town.

"Not sure which instrument to choose?"

Kumiko drew a sharp breath at the sudden voice and looked up. There was Asuka's face, right in front of her. Kumiko was startled enough to jump.

Asuka pushed her glasses up with a finger and stared shamelessly at Kumiko.

"Y-yes?" Kumiko couldn't help but take a step back.

"Except for that one girl, nobody's come over to our section."

"Ah," replied Kumiko, politely noncommittal, which for some reason made Asuka furrow her brow.

The senior in front of Kumiko folded her arms, took a breath, and sighed dramatically. "Except for that one girl, nobody's come over to our section."

"Um, yes. I heard the first time."

"Except for that one girl, nobody's—"

"Um, why do you keep repeating the same thing?" interrupted Kumiko in spite of herself.

Asuka narrowed her eyes and ran her hand back through her hair. "You're pretty dense. I'm obviously inviting you to join my section."

"I-inviting me?"

"That's right. Inviting you." Her lips curled into a smile. "Interested in the euphonium? Right now all we've got in the section is one eupho and a tuba. Every year we're the unpopular ones, which makes it tough…but what do you say? If you don't have something else you want to try for, why not give it a shot?"

"Eupho, huh?"

"That's right. Eupho."

As Kumiko reluctantly struggled for a response, Midori came trotting over, the white bow at her chest swaying. "You're doing bass, too, Kumiko?"

"Huh—?"

"I'm so happy! I was getting kinda worried that there wouldn't be any girls I knew." Midori cocked her head cheerfully. Evidently in her mind it was already certain that Kumiko would be joining the bass section.

"…Fine. I'll do eupho."

"Sweet! Section member secured!" A triumphant Asuka snapped her fingers in victory.

"We're gonna be in the bass section together, so—let's do it, Kumiko!" Midori smiled innocently up at Kumiko.

Behind Midori, Asuka murmured, "…I can use this girl."

"What are you planning, Asuka?" Kumiko asked without thinking.

Asuka turned to look at her and grinned widely. "Me? Oh, nothing."

"…I see." Evidently this particular senior club member was a tough nut to crack.

"Now then, since all the other kids have gone over to their first choice of instruments, we'll just have to wait for the second round."

"So you put students who didn't get their first choice on tuba?"

"We pretty much have to, since there aren't enough applicants. This is a problem for tuba and eupho every year. I dunno why, though—they're such cool instruments."

The bass section hadn't been popular in middle school, either. Students who wanted to join the concert band mostly wanted to play the cool, front-and-center instruments. Kumiko herself had wanted to play the trombone back in elementary school when she'd joined the brass band. She'd adored the way its slide moved in jazz music—but somehow she'd ended up being assigned to the euphonium.

Kumiko looked in Hazuki's direction. Hazuki seemed to be in the middle of some aptitude test. All brass instruments had a mouthpiece that the player blew through. The smaller the instrument, the smaller the mouthpiece—and vice versa. The difference between a tuba's mouthpiece and a trombone's was like the difference between an adult and a child. Unlike woodwinds, brass instruments produced sound when the player vibrated their lips against this mouthpiece.

However, this blowing action was often the first barrier a beginning brass player faced. It was easy enough once you got used to it, but there was technique involved in producing a sound. Simply blowing through the hole as though it were a recorder would get you nowhere. An instrument you could blow and yet still make no sound was a fairly stressful one, and more than a few students seemed intimidated by the prospect.

"Ugh, I can't get a sound!" said Hazuki, holding her instrument and pouting in displeasure. The section leader, Kaori, encouraged her from beside her. The only sounds coming from the bell were the huffs and puffs of Hazuki's breath. It seemed like it might take a day before she was likely to produce a tone.

"Kaori's such a nice section leader," said Midori, impressed.

For some reason Asuka puffed up with pride. "She's the Madonna of the concert band! She's super popular. Everybody loves her."

"Super popular...um, with who?" asked Kumiko hesitantly, even though she felt like she had a pretty good idea of what the answer would be.

"What're you talking about? With the girls, of course!" snickered Asuka.

Kumiko smiled weakly by way of an answer, nodding.

Concert bands were a special place. The ratio of girls to boys was usually around nine to one, but strictly speaking, it was often even more lopsided than that. So it was not uncommon for girls to end up idolizing someone of their own gender. The objects of such infatuated gazes—gazes that were much too fervid to be interpreted as simple envy—tended to either radiate pure femininity or possess a boyish stylishness. Unfortunately, the boys in concert bands were rarely seen as actual boys and so were never the object of such idolization. Kumiko had decided that this was why boys in the band never seemed to have girlfriends, despite being surrounded by girls.

"Tanaka... You're pretty popular yourself, though," said a voice from behind Kumiko.

"Whoa!" said Kumiko, twisting around in surprise at the sudden voice. She turned to see an expressionless Takuya standing right there.

"Is she a definite yes on the eupho?" Takuya asked Asuka, not so much as looking in Kumiko's direction. *You betcha*, nodded Asuka in reply.

"He called you Tanaka...is Asuka your senior, too, Gotou?" Midori tilted her head curiously.

"That's right. He's a second-year student. We've gotten along just fine!"

Hearing this, Kumiko hastily bowed and introduced herself. "Ah, I'm Kumiko Oumae. I'm pleased to meet you!"

"...Gotou," was all he said in response before falling silent again.

Asuka snickered. "My esteemed junior band member is quite shy, so he doesn't talk much. Don't sweat it."

"Ah, okay." Just as Kumiko nodded to show her understanding, a trumpet sounded in the classroom. It was a long, high tone that faded into a soft echo. It had an obvious power unlike any other sounds in the room, and everyone present turned their eyes toward its source.

The person responsible didn't change her expression as she let the trumpet come away from her lips with a casual, easy movement. "...Will that do?" asked Reina Kousaka.

Evidently she'd been asked to play the note as part of a test. A slightly taken-aback Kaori nodded. "Ah, yes."

"Kousaka, you're so good, it's a waste you're attending our school. Which middle school were you?" asked Ogasawara, impressed.

"Kitachu," answered Reina without a smile. "But I also take lessons."

"Wow, so that's why you're so good. I was kinda surprised!"

"Thank you for the kind words. I appreciate it," said Reina with a small bow, though her face didn't show any sign she was pleased. Kumiko got the sense that despite Reina's perfect manners, her expressions were doing her few favors.

"Well, since we've had everybody play, let's go ahead and decide on our trumpets. Let's see…we're limited to three so we'll go with Kousaka, Yoshizawa, and Itoda. Everybody else, move on to your second choices. Let's go, let's go!"

At the club president's behest, the students who didn't make the cut for the trumpet section milled about in the room's empty spaces. Among them, of course, was Hazuki. As Kumiko watched her vaguely, Midori murmured, "Looks like Hazuki didn't get to be a trumpet."

"Too bad."

"Hmm? Midori, are you friends with that girl?" Asuka asked, listening to the pair's conversation as she crept up behind them. Kumiko had a bad feeling about Asuka's pasted-on grin. Midori, however, seemed unconcerned as she nodded affirmatively.

"I see, I see…" said Asuka, stroking her chin and giving Kumiko a meaningful glance. "She didn't do band in middle school, right? She couldn't get a note at all today."

"She said she was in tennis club."

"Oh? So she should have no problem with lung capacity, then," murmured Asuka, placing her hand on Midori's shoulder—that touch alone was enough to bring a bit of color to her cheeks. "What do you say, Midori? Don't you think it'd be fun to have her in our section?"

"I do!"

"Nobody's tried out for tuba yet, and we'll be in a bind if there aren't any takers… Doesn't she look like a tubaist to you? She looks like she has the stamina for it."

"Yeah, maybe Hazuki could be a really good tubaist."

"Would you go over there and invite her? If it comes from a senior like me, she might feel dragged into it, but if it's her friend Midori, she won't feel like she can't say no."

"Okay! I'll go ask her!" replied Midori cheerfully, immediately trotting over to Hazuki. When she got there, she immediately hugged the slack-shouldered girl. From a distance, it looked like Hazuki was still a bit attached to the trumpet, but she would probably cave to Midori's invitation in a matter of minutes.

"…Wow, you've really gotten Midori on your side."

After hearing Kumiko's observation, Asuka let a chuckle slip out. "I'm so happy to have so many adorably agreeable juniors this year."

"'So many'? Don't tell me you're including me in that count."

"Obviously," said Asuka, pushing up her glasses with her index finger. From the other side of those thin lenses, her dark eyes fixed Kumiko in their unreadable gaze. "I can't wait to see how you do, Kumiko."

It was about an hour later by the time everyone's instrument assignments were settled. The Year 1, Class 3 trio of Kumiko, Hazuki, and Midori all landed in the bass section. Reina sat among the trumpet chairs, and Shuuichi was in the trombones, despite having played French horn in middle school.

"Now that we've decided on instruments, I'd like to set the club's direction for this year." Ogasawara cast her gaze around the group. The room was bursting with students, which seemed reasonable for the band's first full meeting. The second- and third-year students busied themselves with languid chatter. There were perhaps eighty people in the room, and their murmurs formed a mass of noise in the room's still air.

"Hey, quiet down! This is a meeting!"

Then, as if to cut Ogasawara off, the sliding classroom door rattled open. "Ah, I see everybody is already here."

"Mr. Taki!" The club president raised her voice happily.

He had a slender, lanky physique, with a well-proportioned musculature that was evident even underneath his shirt. The gentle features of his open, boyish face instantly seized the hearts of every girl in the room. His short-cut black hair sparkled in the light. The brief flash of his white teeth only accentuated his fresh, pleasant charm. Noboru Taki. Thirty-four years old. Homeroom teacher for Year 2, Class 5, and the school's music teacher.

"Wow, it looks like quite a few new students are here. Thirty, perhaps?"

"Twenty-eight."

"So we'll be able to fill all of our empty positions. That's quite a relief," Taki said, then narrowed his eyes in a smile. "I should introduce myself first. I said a few words at the entrance ceremony, so I imagine many of you know who I am, but even so. My name is Noboru Taki, and starting this year I'll be the music instructor at this school. Ordinarily Ms. Matsumoto, who's served as the assistant director to the concert band for many years, would become the new director, but at her request, I've taken the position. I very much look forward to working with you all."

He bowed, looking entirely sincere. Kumiko had never known an adult who treated children with anything apporaching this level of respect. The students' applause filled the music classroom.

Taki looked up, and his expression softened ever so slightly.

"Every year at about this time, I ask a favor of my students," he said, and began to write on the blackboard. The characters were abnormally neat and even, as though he'd typed them on a computer. "It's my policy to value my students' initiative very highly. Therefore, I'd like you all to decide together what your goal is for the year, so I can best help lead you toward it."

Taki pointed to the blackboard, upon which was written *Perform at National Competition.*

"This was your goal last year, wasn't it?"

At Taki's question, an embarrassed-looking Ogasawara bowed her head. "…No, um, Mr. Taki—that wasn't a goal so much as it was, you know…a slogan, or something…it wasn't like we thought we could really go…"

"Ah, I see. Well then, let's not concern ourselves with this," he said lightly, and drew a large X on the blackboard. Its straight, bold strokes seemed to erase the words. As Kumiko watched, it felt somehow difficult to breathe, and she exhaled softly. It was painful. Like her dream had been denied. Suddenly the image of herself in middle school came rushing back to her. *Stupid*, Kumiko spat in self-deprecation. *It's not like you ever seriously thought about trying to get to Nationals.*

"Still, this is a bit of a problem. There's nothing more pointless than setting a goal you don't intend to reach." Taki folded his arms thoughtfully. "I'll follow the goal you set. So if you decide as a class that you'd like to try seriously for Nationals, then practices will be very intense. On the other hand, if you decide that you're happy simply performing and making some fun memories, then there won't be any need for that kind of extreme effort. Personally, I'm happy to take either approach, so please decide for yourselves what you'd like to do."

"We should decide ourselves?" asked the club president, looking a little worried.

That small smile still on his face, Taki nodded.

Please decide for yourselves, he said. Kumiko wondered if this particular adult had any idea how much trouble those simple, pleasant-sounding words really were. She sighed, then furtively glanced around the room, trying to see what her fellow students were thinking—so her opinion wouldn't be the only odd one out.

Ogasawara's gaze fluttered this way and that before finally landing on Asuka, as though she'd suddenly remembered the other girl existed. The leader of the bass section gave a disquieting grin, evidently understanding what was being asked of her.

"Fine, fine. I'll be the secretary," she said, standing.

"That's our vice president!" came a heckle from a corner of the room.

"Wait, Asuka's the vice president?" whispered Hazuki, who sat next to Kumiko.

"Looks like it," Kumiko murmured in reply as she looked in Asuka's direction.

"But how should we decide what our goal's going to be?" said Ogasawara.

"We oughta be able to put it to a vote, right?"

"A vote, huh," said Ogasawara, quirking her head slightly in response to Asuka's proposal. To Kumiko, she looked a bit apprehensive about the idea.

Majority rule. It was the fundamental principle of democracy and one of the ways to decide what action a group would take. And Kumiko, for her part, was not a fan. From the moment she was born, she'd been pushed around by the whims of the majority. The majority was strong and the minority weak. There was strength in numbers, and Kumiko's small voice always seemed to get swallowed up instantly. Fear of being shunned had always kept her from being able to say "no"—just emptying her brain and going along with the crowd. Kumiko sometimes hated that dishonest part of herself.

"I mean, what other way is there?" said Asuka.

"I guess you're right," admitted Ogasawara.

"So what's there to think about? Let's hurry up and do this thang!"

From behind her, Kumiko heard Midori repeat the words "do this thang," as though there was something about them she liked.

Ogasawara silently hesitated, but then with a final murmured "Oh well," she cast her gaze around the room. "All right then, we're going to put it to a vote."

"Leave the counting to me!" said Asuka with a strange note of pride.

"Raise your hand when the goal you prefer is called. The choices will be whether to try for the national competition, or to take it easy and just play in the local ones."

Kumiko put her hand to her cheek in worry. In times like these, usually the right answer had already been decided. Children had to choose the best option from the ones presented by the adults around them—the right answer socially, or globally. The possible options would be naturally narrowed down until you were certain of the correct one.

"Okay, so, people who would like to try for Nationals, please raise your hands."

The students' hands went up together in response. Kumiko, as she raised her own hand, saw the glitter of pink-coated nails in the fluorescent lights and wondered how anyone could play with such long nails. Asuka, seeing an obvious majority of raised hands, stopped writing on the blackboard, presumably because the outcome was obvious.

"Next. People who are satisfied with just going to the Kyoto competition."

A single hand in the middle of the room poked up, a pale white hand sticking out of the dark blue cuff of her blouse. Ogasawara saw who it was, and her breath caught. "Aoi…"

Ogasawara seemed surprised. Her eyes were wide, and her expression made Kumiko hold her own breath.

The person upon whom Kumiko's eyes landed was a very familiar figure indeed.

Aoi Saitou.

"So, just Aoi for the second choice, then," said Asuka, putting a single mark on the blackboard, the lone bar nowhere close to completing a tally of five.

Ogasawara's face contorted in a painful-looking wince, but that, too, lasted but a moment. She brushed her bangs back, then looked at the blackboard with a neutral expression. Asuka's eyes narrowed as though she'd just realized something important.

"By a majority vote," said the club president, "the band's goal will be an appearance at the national competition."

The statement elicited a round of applause from the gathered students, and Taki joined in as well, a pleasant, mild expression on his face, as though he was pleased with the result. As Asuka opened her mouth to speak, he quietly stood and silenced her with a raised hand before looking over the classroom.

"This goal is one you yourselves have chosen. There were some who openly dissented, and I'm sure there were others who, privately, also disagreed. But this is what you have decided together. I will do everything I possibly can to help you reach this goal, but you all must remember this: I can only instruct you. Do not forget that. Without effort from you, your dreams will never become reality. Is that understood?"

At those last words, the classroom fell silent. Why wasn't anybody saying anything? Just as the awkwardness made Kumiko start to squirm, Taki clapped his hands together.

"Why the blank faces? What's your answer?"

A beat after the sharply voiced question from their director, a scattered series of affirmative replies came from the students. *Wait*, Kumiko thought suddenly, frowning. *Have they never practiced responding to the director?*

"Are you awake? I'll ask again. Do you all understand?"

This time, the students' voices rang out as one, filling the room.

"That will be all for today. Good work." The club president's voice rang out cold and clear, bringing the day's band activities to a close. As the murmur of exchanged pleasantries—"Thanks for today!" "See you tomorrow!"—rose in the classroom, Kumiko hastily looked for Aoi. Urgency forced her breath and dried her throat. As soon as she caught sight of a receding form she recognized, Kumiko couldn't help herself from reaching her hand out. "Wait! Ao—um, Saitou!"

Aoi slowly turned to look behind her. Black hair fell over her shoulder in a gentle wave as she did so. As her eyes landed on Kumiko, they widened in sincere surprise. "...Kumiko?"

"Been a while...I mean, it's been quite some time."

The third-year girl laughed slightly at the first-year's halting attempt at polite language. She gently removed Kumiko's hand from her shoulder and looked out the classroom window.

"Want to go home together?"

Kumiko nodded eagerly at the suggestion, as though she were afraid it might get away.

"I didn't know you were going to Kitauji, Aoi."

Aoi smiled softly. Her house was close to Kumiko's, and she'd been like a two-years-older sister. Living in the same neighborhood, they'd often played together when they were in elementary school, but once Aoi had gone on to middle school they hadn't seen much of each other. As a child, Kumiko had always looked up to her, and that hadn't changed. Although Kumiko was now the taller one.

Aoi brushed the black hair she'd always been so proud of aside with her fingertips and nodded in an exceedingly adult manner. "The truth is, I really wanted to go to Horiyama, but I didn't pass the exam."

"Ah, I see." Horiyama was one of the top prep schools in the Kyoto area. Aoi had always been a hardworking, studious girl, which evidently hadn't changed. "Um, can I just talk to you normally instead of being all polite?"

Aoi waved her hand, granting her permission. "Sure, sure! It's really weird to hear my old friend Kumiko being all formal. Although, be polite when other people are around, okay?"

"Sure, gotcha." Kumiko nodded affably at the upperclassman's request.

Aoi put her hand to her mouth as she let slip a quietly refined laugh. The schoolbag slung over her shoulder creaked under its heavy load.

"So, Aoi, why did you raise your hand back there?"

"What do you mean, 'back there'?"

"I mean when they asked whether we wanted to go to Nationals. Nobody was answering seriously anyway, so there really wasn't any need to bother raising your hand, was there?"

Aoi quietly looked down in response to Kumiko's question. Their two shadows fell upon the black asphalt. A chilly spring breeze blew through the space between them. For no particular reason, Kumiko smoothed her uniform's skirt, though it was brand-new and there weren't any wrinkles yet.

"I guess...to have an alibi," said Aoi.

"An alibi?" asked Kumiko.

Aoi smiled with amusement and repeated herself. "That's right, an alibi." From the strap of Aoi's schoolbag dangled a keychain, and Kumiko couldn't decide whether it was cute. The cheap-looking eyes of the deformed little rabbit character stared at her. "So when I quit, I can say that I'd been very clear about my opinion from the beginning."

"Aoi—you're planning on quitting?" Kumiko's voice was suddenly high and pinched-sounding.

Aoi smiled with chagrin at the wide-eyed Kumiko. "Who knows? It's too early to say."

"Why, though? You've kept it up all this time, after all."

"I mean, band stuff won't get you to college." Though her voice was carefully disguised with a casual tone, a glimmer of uneasy self-recrimination peeked out past the façade. The still-untouched textbooks in her bag shifted audibly.

"Where do you want to go to college?" Kumiko asked.

"Who knows. I haven't decided yet."

That's a lie, Kumiko instantly thought. It sounded just as dishonest as that particular kind of conversation students used to protect their fragile sense of self-esteem: *Did you study for the test? No, not at all.* Kumiko pretended not to notice and instead just smiled vaguely. "Ah, okay."

"You should be careful, too, Kumiko. Three years goes by awfully fast." The words echoed against Kumiko's eardrums with an unpleasant tone.

2 ♭I'm Home, Festival♪

The practice space for the bass section was a classroom adjacent to the music room. The writing on the plastic plaque above the door read YEAR 3 CLASS 3, and it was hazy with accumulated dust.

"Bass instruments are so big. I thought I'd try to ease the burden a little, y'know?" said Asuka, stroking her instrument with a finger. The silver euphonium was evidently Asuka's personal instrument, and larger bass instruments could be quite expensive. "Starting in June, practice will be every weekday until seven PM. Come October, we'll end at six thirty. Basically we'll have to start wrapping up when the bell rings."

The schedule was about the same as it had been at Kumiko's middle school. Evidently the routine of weekday practice wouldn't change much in high school.

"Basically, normal practices will be here. We won't do much ensemble practice until a performance is coming up, so in the meantime, practice the sheet music beginning with your instrument's fundamentals."

"How do we do the fundamentals?" asked Hazuki, the complete novice. Midori, meanwhile, seemed mostly uninterested in Asuka's instructions and stared out the window. Takuya was vaguely watching as Midori reached her hand out toward the window, murmuring that she could see the sakura blossoms from here.

"It's things like long tones. Beginners especially need to work on producing a steady sound."

"What's...a long tone?"

"Ah, I'll explain about stuff like that later. First let's introduce everybody." Asuka stood energetically and gave the lectern a hearty smack. Going by the "Ow!" she immediately cried afterward, she'd apparently hit it harder than she meant to. Takuya wordlessly handed her the chill pack from his lunch box. "Uh, so moving right along—introductions!"

A girl who was lying facedown on her desk lifted her head up with sluggish reluctance.

Asuka pointed right between her eyes. "This sleepy so-and-so is Natsuki Nakagawa, second-year eupho!"

"...How's it going." Natsuki, rather impressively, moved her head just from the neck up. The whites of her rather intense eyes were just visible as they flicked up.

"And over here we have Riko Nagase, on the tuba!"

"Hi there," said the girl in question with an affable smile. She seemed quite a bit easier to get along with than the previous upperclassman.

"There are seven of us in the bass section: Me, Gotou, Natsuki, Riko, and the three first-years. Up through last year we had more students on eupho and contrabass, but they graduated or quit."

"It kinda seems like there aren't very many second-year students in the club. It seemed sorta weird to me."

"You think so?" said Kumiko, to which Midori nodded.

"There were thirty-five third-years, eighteen second-years, and twenty-eight first-years...right?"

"That's right—you've got a good memory." Asuka nodded, impressed. It was true—there did seem to be a significant shortage of second-year students in the band.

"Why are there so few?" Kumiko asked, carried away by her own curiosity.

For just an instant, Asuka's dark eyes cooled. Behind the red frames of her glasses, her long eyelashes swept down, then back up. Her lips pursed slightly. "Well—"

"No reason," said Takuya suddenly, cutting Asuka off. "It's nothing first-years need to worry about. You're better off not knowing."

Kumiko flinched away as the much taller boy looked down at her. There was a sharp light in his normally placid eyes. Midori made a small sound as she hid behind Kumiko.

Hazuki alone made a sound of irritation as she pouted. "What's that all about? You're being creepy."

"Hazuki, wait—" started Kumiko, hastily trying to get her to stop.

Natsuki smiled. "Don't worry about it. He just can't stand up to Tanaka, that's all."

"Shut up, Nakagawa." Takuya shot Natsuki a glare.

"Oooh, scary. I'm only telling the truth."

Riko hesitantly tugged on Natsuki's sleeve. Natsuki regarded her classmate briefly, then sniffed in irritation before sulkily flopping over on her desk again. Takuya huffed a resigned sigh, and Riko looked hesitantly over to Asuka. Evidently the second-year students didn't get along very well.

"Now, now, no need for everyone to get all prickly," said Asuka, clapping her hands briskly to clear the air. "Anyway, we've gotten introductions out of the way, so let's pick instruments. I figure nobody already has their own personal instrument?"

"Personal instrument? Do you mean one we own?"

"Yep, yep. Some people do, but usually not in the bass section. A lot of trumpets and flutes do, though."

"Oh, okay," said Hazuki, nodding.

The bass section was packed with large instruments, so students tended not to buy their own, because they couldn't easily bring them home. They were expensive, too, with some costing well over one million yen. Kumiko had always eyed the easily totable flutes and clarinets with envy.

"We keep our instruments in the room next to the music classroom, so now we'll go over and get everybody set up with one," said Asuka as she stood to leave. Kumiko and the others hastily followed.

Directly outside the music classroom was a large sink, and students in the trumpet section were busily washing their mouthpieces there, Reina among them. When she was in middle school, her parents had bought her the gold-plated trumpet she was holding, and it was visibly different from the other students' instruments.

"Oh, Kumiko."

Kumiko stopped at hearing her name called. Reina glanced briefly in Asuka's direction and cocked her head. "Eupho again?"

Kumiko nodded honestly back. "Yup, that's right."

"Hm. Okay," murmured a blank-faced Reina before walking away.

"She a friend of yours?" Hazuki asked.

"Yeah, we went to the same middle school."

"She's a trumpet, right? She's so pretty! Nice chest, too. Easy on the eyes all around!"

Next to Hazuki stood an enchanted Midori, her cheeks blushing red. Hazuki may have been cute, but she sounded like a dirty old man.

Asuka poked her head out of the instrument room and chided the stragglers. "C'mon, stop being silly and get in here!"

Kumiko and the others hurried into the room, whose dusty scent tickled their noses. Hazuki murmured with fascination at the orderly stacks of instruments in their cases. "Whoa, so this is the instrument room?"

"No need to sound so impressed," said Asuka with a sardonic smile. Next to the door were four tuba cases. In the middle of the room, five euphoniums sheepishly huddled in the bottom of some storage shelves, and two contrabasses leaned against the tubas. There were obviously more instruments stored here than they needed, given the size of the band. At some point in the past, the club had probably been larger.

"I've got my own instrument so my case is different, but all the other euphs are the same. Make sure you don't take Natsuki's. Which, by the way, is the one with the weird little bear charm," said Asuka, pointing at one of the cases. And indeed a small, faded yellow bear figurine dangled from it.

At a glance, the black cases all appeared identical, so to avoid problems, the students marked them in various ways. Asuka's instrument case had a blue ribbon tied around its carrying handle.

"I'd recommend the second instrument from the right. The fourth piston's on the bottom so it's easy to press, same as mine. It's gold-plated, although it's pretty well used."

"Oh, okay. I'll use that one, then," said Kumiko, reaching out to take the recommended instrument. Its plating had been worn off here and there, but it was still much nicer than her middle school euphonium had been.

"I'll take this one!" said Midori delightedly as she stood beside Kumiko, who was still closely examining her own instrument. Midori had set her heart on a contrabass. "I'm gonna name him... George!"

"G-George?"

"Yeah! George!" said Midori triumphantly.

Hazuki tilted her head in confusion. "Do you normally name instruments?"

"Sure, why not? It's your precious music partner!"

Hazuki looked doubtfully over to Kumiko.

"Yeah, plenty of people do give them names," said Kumiko.

"George, huh?" said Asuka, folding her arms. "You've got good taste."

"Thank you so much!" said Midori, pressing her palms to her cheeks and sandwiching her face between them bashfully.

Standing between them, Hazuki chose her instrument. "I'll take this one." The tuba case had wheels that made it easier to move, since it was too heavy to just carry around. Hazuki received a thorough lecture from Asuka on how to open the case, and she bobbed her head in serious nods as she took it all in.

She seems happy, thought Kumiko as she took out her own instrument. Unlike Asuka's, it had a sort of sleepy look to it. Kumiko wondered if she ought to name it. She vaguely mulled the idea over, tracing her finger along its surface.

Her still-childish features reflected back at her in the dull golden metal.

"Eupho again?" called out a voice from behind her, shortly after Kumiko had gotten off the train at the Keihan Uji Station. She didn't bother looking back, and soon the sound of trotting footsteps approached. "Aw, c'mon. Why the silent treatment?"

Feeling a hand grabbing her shoulder, Kumiko finally turned to look. It was, of course, Shuuichi. The English vocabulary workbook they'd been given was in his hand, and he was waving at her with it. Kumiko sighed dramatically, her brows knitting slightly. "I'm not ignoring you."

"Liar."

"No, it's true," said Kumiko, closing the paperback book she was holding. Midori had lent it to her. It was a crazy, lurid novel set in Tokyo, about boys and girls in some kind of game being forced to kill each other off in order to survive. Despite her adorably childish features, apparently Midori was crazy for this sort of thing. "Speaking of which, why trombone?"

"What about it?"

"Why'd you pick it? You played French horn in middle school."

"Ah." Shuuichi chuckled. The thick workbook in his hand wobbled. Kumiko watched the cheap fluorescent price tag quiver. She realized there would be a test tomorrow and exhaled quietly.

"I always wanted to play the trombone more than the horn. In middle school we played rock-paper-scissors for it, and I lost. But this time, I won."

"I think the horn's good, too, though."

"Yeah, I liked it fine, but c'mon—the trombone's just so cool!"

"I guess it is." Kumiko liked the trombone herself. Unlike all the other brass instruments, it had a slide the player used to adjust the pitch. There was something appealing about that particular trait.

"Reina's doing trumpet again. Just like in middle school."

"Oh, Kousaka? Well, she was always obsessed with the trumpet." Shuuichi had been in the same middle school concert band as Reina. That said, they weren't especially close, being only acquaintances at best. The middle school band had had nearly a hundred members, so many of them knew little more than the names of their fellow students. So long as they weren't in your section, there wasn't much need to get to know them. "I don't know. I get kind of a weird vibe from the Kitauji band."

"Really?" said Kumiko, cocking her head curiously. She'd only done one sectional practice so far but hadn't felt anything particularly awkward in the bass section.

Shuuichi's shoulders drooped, and his gaze flicked over Uji River as though searching for an escape. The setting sun scattered flecks of brilliance across the river's surface. He straightened, seemingly trying to peer into the river's depths, but the water was too dark to see into. "Well, sure, you're in the Bass Kingdom. That's Tanaka's territory."

"What the heck's the 'Bass Kingdom'?"

"I don't really know, either, but some of the seniors were talking about it. That since Tanaka rules it, it will never fall."

"Does that mean the other sections will?"

"Look, just between you and me," said Shuuichi with an exhausted-looking smile, "there are hardly any second-years in the Kitauji band, right? Do you know why?"

"Oh yeah, we started to talk about that over lunch. But Gotou made us stop."

It's nothing first-years need to worry about, he'd said. Kumiko couldn't help but sigh at the memory. He'd been obviously displeased. Was the topic really so upsetting?

"Yeah, apparently they had a huge fight with the third-years. There used to be over thirty of them, but something like half of them dropped out, I guess."

"What'd they fight over?"

"You'll never believe it," said Shuuichi. Whatever it was, it had him fairly worked up. His normally half-lidded eyes were wide with excitement. "It's really frustrating, but none of the third-years were practicing! Even though they all sucked! And they had the nerve to yell at the first-years not to ditch practice. So that was why the second-years—well, they were first-years, then, but—that's why they had this crazy problem with their seniors."

"Really?" was all Kumiko could say in response. She'd never picked up on anything like that in the bass section. Asuka, a third-year student, loved the eupho more than anyone else and would happily—for whatever reason—play it nonstop. If anything, it felt like the second-year, Natsuki, would be the obvious candidate for skipping practice.

Kumiko said so, at which Shuuichi smiled in surrender. "Yeah, well, Tanaka's another story. The president, and Kaori, too. They're all exceptions."

"Kaori—you mean the trumpet?"

"Yeah. She's really nice, really hot, and practices like crazy. I wonder if we could trade our section leader for her," said Shuuichi with a serious face. "I know Mr. Taki's talking about going to Nationals, but I bet it'll be impossible so long as those third-years are around. They're holding everybody back. Even though the new first-years are all really good." With a faraway gaze, he murmured, "Man, I really wanna go to Nationals just once."

Kumiko wondered if he was thinking about their middle school competition. Despite having set an appearance at Nationals as their goal, Kitachu had only made it to the regional level. They'd done their absolute best, but their dreams had failed to come true. The reality was that only a handful of people ever saw their efforts come to anything. The children who slipped free from God's hand became cynically calculating as their failures piled up. There was no need to stand and fight—you could just run away. It was an easier way to live.

Kumiko exhaled softly to avoid her own thoughts. If your efforts were never going to be rewarded, there was no point in working hard to begin with. You could save yourself the pain. Playing just well enough, having a little bit of fun—what was wrong with a band like that? But there was no way she could say anything like that to Shuuichi.

Every year in May, all the various high school concert bands in Kyoto would assemble for a parade in Taiyou Park. The bands would perform while marching around the spacious facility. The park hosted a variety of musical events, and the marching festival was an established annual tradition.

"The...SunFest?" asked Hazuki, her head tilted curiously and her arms wrapped around a tuba that seemed in no danger of making any noise.

"That's right." Asuka nodded. They were at the day's after-school sectional practice. "To be more specific, the Twenty-Third Annual Sunrise Festival."

Midori nodded. "They've been doing it for twenty-three years," she added, sounding impressed. She was expertly applying rosin to her bow.

The bow was strung with horsehair, which tended to slip over the bass's strings, and it was this rosin—a solid substance made from sticky pine resin—that gave the hair good traction. Without rosin, the bow would just glide over the strings and produce no noise at all. Beginners tended to have trouble knowing how much rosin to use, often applying too much, which resulted in a dry, rustling tone.

"Have we decided on music yet?"

Asuka nodded grandly in response to Takuya's question. "Yup. Here," she said, handing out sheet music. The title: "Can't Buy Me Love."

"This year, only the first-year students who already have experience with their instruments will be performing, so no sheet music for you, Hazuki."

"Oh, okay," said Hazuki, the sole nonrecipient of the new music. Her shoulders sagged a little.

Kumiko suddenly felt vaguely villainous for having received sheet music. She shared a private look with Midori. Still, Hazuki couldn't yet produce a proper tone from her tuba, so Asuka's decision was understandable.

"What's Hazuki going to do for the festival?"

Natsuki grinned. "Oh, y'know—the annual mystery march."

"M-mystery march...?" Hazuki looked uncertainly to Kumiko.

"Don't worry about it. You just have to carry pom-poms and march behind the band," said Riko with a reassuring smile.

"Pom-poms..." murmured Hazuki, looking increasingly uneasy.

Takuya watched Hazuki worriedly. He'd opened, then closed his mouth several times during the conversation. Apparently he didn't have much of a way with words.

"There aren't many beginners in our section this year, but there's lots in the other sections, so don't worry. Last year Riko and Natsuki were marching."

"You guys were beginners?" Relief softened Hazuki's expression.

"Yeah," nodded Natsuki. "Riko's so unathletic that she never really got the marching part down, though."

"C'mon! You didn't have to bring that up!" said Riko, face reddening as she smacked Natsuki's back.

"Ha-ha, sorry, sorry."

After coming to band practice for several days, Kumiko had realized that Riko and Natsuki didn't get along too badly. Or rather, they *did* get along—and quite well. Somehow they'd seemed sort of tense at first, but apparently that had been Kumiko's misunderstanding. Why had it seemed that way, that first day? She thought back to their first sectional practice and rubbed her chin. It had only been a few days, but the memory was already becoming vague, and try as she might to catch it, it slipped from her grasp.

"So, what kind of song is 'Can't Buy Me Love'?"

Asuka's eyes lit up at Hazuki's question. *Aw, crap*, thought Kumiko—but Asuka had already started talking.

"So, this is a jazz-style arrangement of a single that hit the charts in March 1964, from a British band called the Beatles. You've at least heard them played in English class and stuff, right? Now, this version of 'Can't Buy Me Love' doesn't start with the original's intro, but instead comes on strong right where Paul McCartney would be singing the title line. British presales for the single topped a million copies, with two million presold in America, making it the first single in history to sell more than one million copies on reservation alone. Also—"

"Okay, okay. I'll read the rest on Wikipedia later." Takuya's interruption brought Asuka's rapid-fire monologue to a halt. Asuka was a very good leader, but Kumiko wished that she would do something about her tendency to get started talking and become impossible to stop.

Asuka shrugged. "Well, anyway, we've got about a month, so I think it'll be fine. Once this is over, it'll be smooth sailing on to the competition."

"The competition," groaned Takuya. "I wonder how it'll go this year." He looked out the window. From the third-floor classroom, all they could see was thickly overgrown greenery, thanks to the large, forested hill that sat directly behind the school. Stirred by the breeze, the blossoms quivered as though giggling at some joke about the students they watched. The sun had been out in full force just moments earlier but now hid behind a cloud, its brilliant rays suddenly dimmed. A moist scent tickled Kumiko's nose. There would be rain soon.

"Mr. Taki told us to assemble for practice after we can properly play together as an ensemble. I figure we've been given about a week, tops, so let's do our best until then."

"Okay," nodded Kumiko in response.

Ensemble practice. What kind of instruction would Noboru Taki give?

Something about his features—or maybe his gentle demeanor—made him very popular with students. Especially the girls. His regular-curriculum music class was widely coveted, and any student who got into it considered themselves lucky. Kumiko's homeroom teacher, Michie, was also fairly popular. She had the bizarre nickname "Ms. Drill Sergeant," and while she came off as unbelievably strict, she was known for being very nice to students who took their work seriously. The concert band had lucked out in its faculty directors. Even students in other clubs and teams at Kitauji said so. Kumiko had never seen Mr. Taki teach before, but she was sure it was going to be a lot of fun. Though she had no evidence, she held the certainty in her mind as she blew through her mouthpiece. Her instrument vibrated, loosing a long, penetrating note.

The first ensemble practice was held on a Sunday, about a week after they'd been given their sheet music. Before the practice could start, the desks and chairs in the music room had to be moved into the hallway, in order to fit the club's eighty-odd students and their music stands, plus the various percussion instruments. Kumiko and the others in her section brought a small platform up from the instrument storage room and arranged it in the bass section's corner of the music room. Woodwind instruments were in the front, with brass in the back, and the various percussion instruments at the edges, situated such that they could see the conductor. Since the music classroom had no soundproofing, they hung old blankets from the walls to provide some semblance of deadening, since the cloth absorbed sound.

The beginner students hadn't gotten to where they could properly play their sheet music yet, but since this was the first ensemble practice, they were attending along with the rest of the band—not to play, but to watch and learn.

"Today is our first ensemble practice," said Taki with a smile as he took his seat at the front, facing the students. Kumiko quietly tried to calm her nerves as she fidgeted with the bucket by her foot with the tip of her shoe. Her heart was pounding. She'd been in countless ensemble practices during middle school, but this was her first time in high school.

"So, did you all do as I asked? Did you practice well enough to play as an ensemble?"

Taki's question was answered by an uneven scattering of student voices. Taki wore a somewhat pained smile, then picked up his baton. "Well, then. We'll start by tuning."

At his direction, the band members played a tone. After practicing some simple basics for a while, they moved on to "Can't Buy Me Love."

Taki raised his baton. The band all held their instruments ready. Kumiko, too, took up her eupho. She readied her fingers over the valves and felt a chill.

Taki took a breath, then called out in a clear voice. "One, two, one, two, three, four—"

The percussion section laid down the song's rhythm as Taki's baton sliced down, and the brass sounded, sending their notes flying over the beat. The uptempo song made you want to just get up and start moving. Kumiko's eyes followed the baton with intense focus.

The band played well up until the middle, but halfway through, the brass section fell out of sync with the percussion section's rhythm. The slight incongruity blossomed, and all at once the various parts fell into disarray. The melody scattered into clashing notes. Bass and treble parted ways over irreconcilable differences. The messy sound could no longer even generously be described as "music."

"Okay, that's enough." Taki forcibly brought the playing to a halt. Students removed their mouths from their instruments, embarrassed smiles on their faces. They were all perfectly aware there was nothing to be proud of in what they'd just played.

Kumiko, too, rested her instrument in her lap. "Ugh, that was awful," she heard Natsuki murmur.

"What was that?" asked Taki, his faint smile still in place as he tilted his head curiously. His voice was as calm as it always was, but there was a faint, sharp edge to it now. Kumiko could practically feel the temperature in the room drop.

"President."

Ogasawara scrambled wildly as she summoned an answer. "Y-yes! Um, what?"

"My instructions were clear, weren't they? That you were only to assemble once your playing was at a level where you could perform as an ensemble."

"Y-yes. You did say that."

"And this is the result?" Taki's expression had not changed, which made it worse. Ogasawara seemed somehow even smaller than she already was. Kumiko could hear Natsuki swallow nervously next to her.

"What do you all think ensemble practice is for?"

Nobody answered the director's question. An unpleasant silence fell over the room. Taki sighed with exasperation, then pointed to the trombone section. "What do you think?"

"M-me?" the chosen student stammered, obviously rattled. The familiar voice obviously belonged to Shuuichi. "Um, isn't it so we can practice playing together the way we would for a real performance...?"

"Right. That's what I think, too."

Shuuichi sighed in relief, perhaps heartened to hear agreement from Taki. But the nervous energy in the classroom had not dissipated. Kumiko's stomach clenched from the weight of it, and she bit her lip.

"But we can't practice as an ensemble like this. Each part is too riddled with faults. An ensemble can recover from a small mistake, but when your playing is this poor, the piece itself simply falls apart. Aren't you embarrassed to be performing this badly when you play as an ensemble?"

The students recoiled at the openly harsh criticism.

"I hadn't thought this was the extent of your ability. It's disgraceful."

At this, a student toward the back of the room stood up. A third-year trombone. "Now wait just a minute. I don't think it's fair to talk to us like that."

Taki gave the student a look. He chuckled softly through his nose, his slight smile unmoved. "Is that so?"

"It's not like we were just playing around, and we did practice!"

"You weren't playing around? I see," Taki said and quietly narrowed his eyes. With a slow, deliberate movement, he plucked the baton from the lectern. He turned around the metronome sitting there and adjusted the tempo. When he pulled his hand away, it began to sound a quick tempo: *tick, tick, tick.*

"Trombones, I'd like you to begin playing to the metronome from where you come in. It's okay to ignore the percussion parts. Understood?"

The trombone players readied their instruments. Taki waited until their bells were all raised, then counted off. "One, two, three, four—"

The melody arrived on his count. The section's playing was scattershot right from the start. There were probably several players in the section whose timing was off.

Taki didn't so much as raise his eyebrow at the messy performance. "Thank you, that's enough."

The trombones uneasily lowered their instruments at his cue.

"What do you all think of this performance?"

Taki's gaze swept through an arc covering the entire classroom, but nobody met his eyes. He sighed and smiled a somewhat frustrated smile. "My thought was 'This isn't just the trombones.' The other sections are just as incapable of even playing as a unit to support their parts' performance. Why do you imagine that is?"

The stifling, tense atmosphere of the classroom clung to Kumiko's skin.

"I made sure to come and visit each of your sectional practices over the past week. You all seemed to be having a delightful time. I could hear your chatting echoing in the halls. There were some rooms where I didn't hear a single instrument playing."

Students in the sections around her wore decidedly uncomfortable expressions on their faces. Apparently Taki had hit the bull's-eye. Kumiko suddenly remembered her conversation with Shuuichi the previous week. Apparently it was just like he'd said—Kitauji's concert band didn't take practice all that seriously.

"I don't necessarily want you to kill yourselves practicing. But you were the ones who decided that you wanted to make it to Nationals. So this is a problem. You must be able to achieve basic preparation for ensemble performance during your sectional practices. This is quite troubling," he said, spitting the words out evenly, despite the smile he still wore. "I don't know what it is that you've misunderstood, but I don't come to school on my days off just to play around with you all. I come to teach. So what is this, then? The performance you just gave is not even ready for my instruction. And I would prefer not to waste my precious weekends."

Kumiko heard a girl's sniffling sobs from a corner of the classroom. Taki's expression, nevertheless, was unmoved. His eyes assumed the form of a smile, but their color was cold—cold enough to send chills down Kumiko's spine.

"President."

"Y-yes?" Ogasawara's voice cracked, but nobody laughed.

"It's only two, but I'm ending today's ensemble practice. Please practice as sections for the rest of your time today."

"Understood."

"Also, parent-teacher meetings begin next week, which means classes will end at noon. That will give you all plenty of time to practice, so I'll be scheduling the next ensemble for Wednesday at two. Will that do?"

"O-of course!"

"All right. Everyone, please make sure your playing is at basic ensemble level by then. Is that understood?"

There was no answer. The band was frozen, unmoving. Taki's smile never wavered as he spoke again. "Your response?"

This prompted a scattered, hesitant "Yes, sir," from the assembled students. Kumiko said nothing. The two simple words caught in her throat. Her mouth was dry from nerves.

Taki collected his sheet music and left the classroom. Nobody moved. Nobody said anything. A strange silence had fallen over them. For some reason, Kumiko grabbed her own wrist and squeezed. She looked at the white marks left behind on her slightly tanned skin, finally exhaling as she did so. Her wrist hurt a little.

After a fair amount of time had passed since Taki had left the classroom, a single student finally stood.

"What's *his* problem?"

It was one of the seniors, a French horn, who had finally cut the tension restraining the room. Immediately after her remark, students filled the room with one complaint after another.

"He's, like, so annoying."

"What was that even? So awkward."

"Pisses me off. What's the point?"

Grievances clouded the air, becoming a din that thrummed against Kumiko's eardrums. Her brow reflexively furrowed.

From the center of the room, Asuka took charge. "All right, all right! Enough complaining! Everybody head back to their section's practice rooms! It's time to practice, practice, practice!" At her feet was crouched a seemingly withered Ogasawara. Kumiko wondered which one of them was supposed to be the club president.

"C'mon, Kumiko, let's get going," prompted Hazuki, slapping Kumiko on the back, and they headed out of the music classroom.

Kumiko glanced over her shoulder and met the eyes of Reina, who was hugging her trumpet as though it were something gravely important. Fringed with long lashes, her lovely eyes glittered obsidian. And for some reason, they seemed to smolder with rage.

There were a variety of routes from Keihan Uji Station to Kumiko's home. Typically she took the shortest route, crossing Uji Bridge and continuing along Byoudou-in Avenue. Today, however, she didn't feel like it. *Aren't you embarrassed?* Taki's words to the concert band continued to smolder in Kumiko's heart. The heaviness of it seemed enough to collapse her lungs, and movement itself felt oppressive. On days when she was this depressed, Kumiko always made a stop before going home.

She exited the station and walked alongside the river, and soon the entrance of Uji Shrine came into view. To the right of the *torii* gate could be seen the vermilion-painted Asagiri Bridge, and at its entrance was a small monument: a statue of a man and a woman wearing kimono and sitting in repose. They were the Lady Ukifune and Prince Niou, from *The Tale of Genji*. This area of Kyoto had been the setting for the final ten chapters of the literary classic, hence the monument commemorating them. That said, Kumiko had only ever read the excerpts of *The Tale of Genji* that showed up in her school textbooks, so she had no idea who Ukifune or Niou were.

Kumiko sat down on the river's embankment and stretched her legs. Gazing at the brilliant red of the Asagiri Bridge, she felt suddenly apathetic about it all. The river's quiet murmur held a peaceful stillness that was decidedly comforting. Time seemed to slow, and the second hand of her wristwatch seemed to tick out each second only with great reluctance.

"Hey," called a voice. Kumiko looked up. It was Shuuichi. "What's with the dirty look?" He frowned and sat beside her without asking. Wrinkles stood out on his uniform's black slacks.

"What're you doing here?" asked Kumiko.

"Probably the same thing you are. Change of scenery."

"Mm." It seemed a suspicious coincidence to Kumiko, but she couldn't think of anything to say, so she pursued the topic no further. Instead she said the first thing that did come to mind. "Mr. Taki was pretty scary."

"Man, that was rough. He's terrifying," said Shuuichi with a chuckle. He combed his hand back through his hair, his shoulders slackening. "Our section leader flipped out on him. Guess she got what she deserved, though."

Kumiko leaned forward onto her knees. Thinking about what was going to happen next with the band made her extremely gloomy. "I wonder if he really thinks we can go all the way to Nationals."

"Honestly, it's probably impossible, at our level. It's, like, people have to get their heads out of the clouds. And the third-years just chat all the way through sectional practices. Aiming that high is just embarrassing," he muttered, his lips curling cynically. "He might be teaching us, but who knows if he's even any good."

"Yeah. He did say this was his first time as director."

"He's great, obviously! Are you kidding?"

Kumiko and Shuuichi turned around, startled by the sudden voice. Being caught in the act of gossiping about someone was always awkward.

Standing there glaring at the two of them and full of righteous indignation was Reina. Her trumpet case hung from her left hand.

"What're you doing here...?" Reina had gone to the same middle school as Kumiko for three years, but she'd never encountered Reina here in her own neighborhood.

Standing behind them, Reina looked down at Kumiko and Shuuichi with an irritated expression and sniffed. "I live around here. By Ujigami Shrine."

"I've never seen you around..."

"Probably because I don't take the train. I've *always* ridden my bike to school."

"O-oh," said Kumiko, somewhat cowed. Shuuichi, meanwhile, was stiff as a board. Kumiko remembered that he had a terrible time dealing with any girls other than her.

"So? What were you two talking about?" Reina loomed over her and leaned down close.

Kumiko reflexively looked away. Having a beautiful girl get in her face like this was bad for her heart. "Um, I mean..."

Angling to deliver a finishing blow to the flailing Kumiko, Reina took another step closer. Shuuichi's face went white. "I'll have you know that Mr. Taki is amazing! I won't let you make fun of him!"

"O-okay."

Reina then snagged Shuuichi in her gaze. "You too—are you listening?"

He cowered before the spear point of her eyes.

"Your response?"

"Y-yes."

"That's more like it," nodded Reina, satisfied. The imperious beauty, still holding her trumpet case, turned her attention back to Kumiko. "I'll let it go this time, but I won't forgive you for bad-mouthing Mr. Taki again in the future."

"W-we weren't really bad-mouthing, we just..."

Hearing Shuuichi's halfhearted defense, Reina flicked her sharp gaze back to him. Her pale pink lips curled into a sneer. "Were you saying something?"

"Uh, n-no, nothing…" The boy raised a white flag.

"So long as we're understood. See you," said Reina, striding off as though nothing had happened.

Kumiko wondered where her fury had come from. The area around them was suddenly quiet again. She and Shuuichi just stared at each other for a few moments, then finally stood.

"…Let's go home."

"Yeah."

A swell of innocent laughter rose from a group of boys running along the embankment's path. Kumiko felt suddenly fatigued and rubbed the corners of her eyes. Shuuichi gazed down at her as though he wanted to say something, but in the end he remained silent.

The next day, when Kumiko walked through the door to the classroom where her sectional practice was held, she was surprised to encounter Mr. Taki.

"Good day, Miss Oumae."

"Oh, um, hello!" Kumiko scrambled to bow properly in response to Taki's polite nod. Apparently he'd already memorized his students' names.

"Kumiko, today Mr. Taki's going to be leading our practice, so hurry up and get set up," explained Asuka.

"Ah—okay! I will." Kumiko hastily made for the instrument storage room. She took the euphonium that she was finally getting used to out of its case and pulled her folder of sheet music off the shelf. The standard music folder for the band had antireflective transparent sheet protectors inside it—reflections during concerts could make the music difficult to read.

By the time Kumiko returned to the bass section's practice room, most of the rest of the section had already assembled. "Sorry to keep you waiting!" she said. The only one missing was Hazuki, who was absent thanks to her parent-teacher meeting.

"Feel free to sit where you usually do."

"Ah, all right." Kumiko hurried to her seat.

Taki looked over the gathered students, and his expression suddenly softened. "I came today to hear what sorts of sounds you're producing on your instruments. Unfortunately, I have parent-teacher meetings beginning at four o'clock, so I hope you'll help me see where you are before I have to leave. Is that understood?" Taki looked to Asuka.

The bass section leader smiled her always-crafty smile and answered with a hearty "Yes!"

"All right. First of all, I'd like you to sing your tuning together."

Tuning, simply put, was the act of adjusting the pitch of an instrument. Unless this was properly done, instruments that ought to be playing the same note would instead produce dissonant tones that collided unpleasantly with one another. When the entire band played the same long note together, a wobbling, vibrating sound was proof that their tuning wasn't correct. This wasn't something that you had to worry about while listening to music, but for performing, the issue of correct pitch was of critical importance. Incidentally, the euphonium was tuned by pulling out or pushing in a length of tubing.

"Sing...?" asked Riko.

"Yes, that's right," said Taki with a nod.

Next to him, Asuka stroked her chin. "Mr. Taki, are you by any chance planning to introduce solfège into your instruction?"

"Very astute, Miss Tanaka," said Taki, seemingly impressed.

Natsuki tilted her head, mystified. "Sol-what? What's that?"

"Solfège is a form of basic music training that emphasizes sight-singing. Before we begin practice, I thought I'd have you try singing a few of the songs from the textbook I'm about to hand out. This kind of drill will improve your sight-reading and pitch sensitivity."

"I did this kind of practice in middle school, too!" said Midori excitedly from where she sat next to Kumiko. If the powerhouse Seijo school practiced like this, then maybe there was something to it.

"That said, since we're a bit short on time today, I thought we'd start with tuning and see how that goes," said Taki. He played a B flat on his laptop. "I'd like to have each of you sing this note in turn, clockwise."

"Okay." Asuka nodded, then sang in tune with the note that was playing. Though she was a girl, Asuka's voice had a low, mellow quality that flustered Kumiko a bit just listening to it.

After her, each student sang in turn. Kumiko assumed that all of them would have some basic aptitude for music, since they had already joined the concert band, but—

"...Gotou, is it possibly the case that singing is not your forte?"

Takuya looked gloomily away at Taki's obliquely worded question. Evidently he was moderately tone-deaf, since his singing voice possessed considerable destructive potential.

Taki smiled wryly. "Don't worry. It may seem unfamiliar now, but once you get the hang of it you'll get better and better. Let's give it a shot, shall we?"

"O-okay." Takuya was thoroughly deflated, his big body hunched over.

Asuka cackled and smacked him on the back. "Don't sweat it! I know someone even more tone-deaf than you."

"Who's that?" Kumiko asked.

"Haruka," answered Asuka lightly.

"The president *is* incredibly bad at singing," murmured Natsuki, sounding as though she spoke from experience.

"Setting aside the issue of who's more tone-deaf than whom, now I'd like you to try playing the same note on your instruments."

The students played the tone one by one. Oddly enough, Takuya had no trouble producing the correct tone on his instrument, despite his catastrophic singing performance.

"Now, this time, you'll play together. The same note as before."

Everyone did as instructed and played a B flat. The bass notes overlapped, producing a distinctly wobbling sound against the note coming from the computer. They were out of tune.

"Try to concentrate on making the computer's tone disappear into your instrument's sound. Don't just blow through your instrument, make it part of the sounds around it."

Make the tone disappear into your sound. Kumiko concentrated on the words and listened carefully to the sounds around her. They rippled, blending together, and the quavering slowly faded. Euphonium, tuba, and contrabass. The timbres of the three instruments melted together, forming a single spirit. And just then, Kumiko heard a high tone that seemed impossible. It was an F—almost like a French horn would make.

"There, that's enough."

At Taki's signal, Kumiko lowered her instrument. It was the most beautiful unison she'd heard them manage to play so far. Back in middle school their teachers had lectured them endlessly about pitch, but this was the first time she'd paid such close, serious attention to it.

"Did you all hear that F?"

The bass section's members all nodded.

"That was the harmonic overtone. It's much easier to hear when you're playing together in tune. If you can attain this sound while performing, it has the same harmonic effect as playing in just intonation. It can be quite difficult to stay in tune, but a beautiful ensemble performance is simply impossible otherwise. Ensemble playing isn't about simply demonstrating brilliant instrumental skill—the beauty of a band's performance comes from the layering of each sound, which means that when playing together, you must listen to each part in the ensemble around you and adjust to match."

"Yes, sir!" replied Kumiko and her bandmates energetically. Despite the brief instruction, she felt like they'd grasped how to play in tune. She wanted to try playing this way with the rest of the concert band as soon as she could.

Taki's eyes narrowed in a smile, as though reading Kumiko's mind. "So, before I go, shall we try playing something together, just as the bass section?" he said, picking up his baton.

The day of the band's second ensemble practice there was a strangely heightened nervous energy among the students. Even the seniors who'd last time just chatted and hung out until Taki arrived were now all carefully scrutinizing their sheet music. Kumiko set her folder on her music stand and got her tuner out of her pocket.

Tuning was something that absolutely had to be done before any concert band ensemble practice. Put simply, it was the process of adjusting an instrument's pitch. The tuner was a device used to accomplish this, and Kumiko had bought one for three thousand yen in middle school. Tuners ranged from cheap to wildly expensive—mechanical strobe tuners often cost upward of five hundred thousand yen. When Kumiko brought her tuner close to her horn's bell and played a note, its little display told her whether the note was sharp or flat. Other tuners would simply play the correct note themselves, which the user would listen to and then adjust their instrument to match.

The president stood at the front of the room and led the band through a final ensemble tuning. They all played the same note, then adjusted their instruments sharp or flat. Brass instruments tended to play sharper in warmer environments and lower when the temperature fell. When it came time to perform in a competition, they would have to consider not only the location's weather, but also the venue's air conditioning and the travel time to get there as well. The ability to consider minute details like these was what separated the schools with high-level bands from the rest.

"Everybody's pretty hyped today," chuckled Natsuki, sitting next to Kumiko. Natsuki had her sheet music at hand, and Kumiko noticed some handwritten notes on it here and there that hadn't been there before.

"Well, nobody wants to get yelled at like last time."

"Yeah. I don't think that's the only reason, though," said Natsuki, looking over to the edge of the classroom.

A group of third-year students had clustered there, murmuring secretively to each other. Snippets of their conversation cut through the horn sounds in the room, unmistakably audible—*I hate that guy. We'll show him.* According to rumor, Taki had put in after-school appearances at every section's practice over the past few days, and apparently he had delivered some rather harsh words during some of them. There had been several sightings of students reduced to tears as they tried to play.

"Looks like there are some grudges," said Kumiko.

"They're just assholes."

At Natsuki's harsh pronouncement, Kumiko reflexively looked around, but fortunately it seemed like nobody had overheard. "Natsuki, I really think it would be better if you didn't say stuff like that so loudly..."

"What? It's true," said Natsuki, completely unapologetically. "I mean, don't you agree?"

"Wha—" Kumiko began to stammer, but she was saved from having to say anything further by the arrival of their fresh-faced director. The noisy classroom instantly quieted.

Taki took a seat at the front of the room and opened his conductor's score. The eyes of the entire band were on him. His own beleaguered gaze fell to the sheet music in front of him, but he looked back up as something seemed to occur to him. His kind-seeming eyes swept once over the classroom.

"It looks like everyone is here," he said mildly. "So—do you feel like you're playing a bit better?"

"We've definitely improved," said the president.

Taki narrowed his eyes in a smile. "I see. Well, let's make sure you're all properly tuned, then. And as you play, please keep in mind what you learned during this week's sectionals," he said, then played a B flat on the classroom's organ.

He then gave his baton a light wave, and the band all played the same note together. A clear, pure sound filled the room—totally unlike what had happened at the previous practice. There was no wobbling in pitch, and the sound's superior fullness was immediately obvious. The way they were playing itself felt different, as each instrument's tone had utterly changed. The instruments themselves sang.

"Thank you," said Taki, bringing the baton down. At the gesture, Kumiko and the rest of the band all stopped playing. The dramatic change in their sound over such a short period of time had to be because of Taki's instruction. As the band saw so clearly the fruits of their own improvement, a chattering murmur rose among them, their cheeks flushed with excitement.

Taki clapped his hands to silence the clamor. "I can see that you're all very happy, but band practice is not the time for personal chatter. Let's move on to fundamentals. We'll start by playing number three from the sheet music you've been given."

Fundamentals practice continued for some time thereafter. Kumiko wondered why, if they'd assembled in order to practice their SunFest piece, they were doing so much of these tedious basic drills. And she didn't seem to be the only one who was thinking the same thing—Kumiko noticed many bored-looking faces around her. But then there was Asuka, who fixed the band director firmly in her gaze as she played the simple pieces with a serious expression on her face.

"Suzuka, on clarinet—you're a bit sharp."

"Ah—thank you."

Kumiko rested her chin in her hands as she thought it over. What was with Taki's ears? Even listening to the entire band playing at once, he could accurately catch the slightest mistake in playing.

"...All right. Let's try playing 'Can't Buy Me Love.'"

Hearing this, the students—thoroughly bored with practicing fundamentals—all looked up. Taki readied his baton with a wan smile. And all the instruments that had been laid down now faced forward.

"One, two, one, two, three, four..." He brought his baton down, and the drums started playing the rhythm. Then the brass and woodwinds added the melody, and the music's cheer intensified. The song used a brisk tempo, but once they'd grasped the feel of it, it would carry them through to the end. Kumiko followed the sheet music intently, putting everything she had into keeping up with the notes' fingerings. Even as the many sounds threatened to tangle, the baton whipped them free. Even as the flute runs and trumpet melodies stumbled, or the percussion and bass sections ran into problems, the tune went on. And then when they reached the finalé—the baton froze.

...It's finally over. Kumiko was sure she wasn't the only person thinking as much. She spotted relieved sighs all around her. She was shockingly tired—playing in her middle school ensemble had never demanded such concentration or been so exhausting.

Taki closed his eyes in thought for a brief, quiet moment. His lips softened. With a long, slender finger, he flipped through his sheet music. "Well, I suppose we can call that a passing grade."

Asuka knitted her brow. While the performance they'd just given was clearly superior to last week's, evidently it still wasn't the level Taki was looking for.

"Your performance will be in early May. We do not have many days left to practice. And the SunFest is a parade. You will need to memorize this music and perform it while marching. Are you confident you'll be able to do so?" said Taki provocatively, looking over the classroom. The band's eyes were downcast to avoid meeting his gaze.

"Well, I am. Confident, that is," he finished.

Kumiko blinked at Taki's statement.

He picked up a stack of papers from his desk and handed them to the clarinets in the front row to pass back to the rest of the band. On the cheap, newsprint-like paper, there was a rigorously detailed practice regimen.

Natsuki couldn't help but scowl at the schedule's precision. "Ugh, are you kidding me?" she mumbled.

Hearing this, Kumiko took another look at her own copy. It described in minute detail not only how to do fundamental practice but also how they should carry out their sectional practices. Fitting it all in would make for a seriously difficult schedule.

"Um, Mr. Taki," said Ogasawara, as though she couldn't help speaking up. "Are we really going to do all of these practices?"

"Why wouldn't you?" said Taki, his head tilted curiously. "I would think that if you use all the time you fritter away on simply being young, this amount of practice would be no problem. You should be able to complete it within the time you've spent on club activities so far. Oh, of course the first-year beginners have a different course of practice, so make sure to keep that in mind."

His expression was gentle, but what he was saying was quite severe. Next to the president, Aoi stared down at the practice schedule, her sax hanging from her neck. On the palm of her right hand was a math formula written in red pen. She wondered what the scribble on Aoi's palm was and whether she herself would someday have to memorize something like it. Kumiko held her aching head in her hands.

"The SunFest is where schools from all over the area display their skill. I will not accept the sort of careless performance this band has given in previous years. From now on, I want you to take each and every public performance very seriously."

"It's not like we've just been screwing around up until now," somebody murmured, but Taki overlooked the grumble with a smile.

Natsuki chuckled through her nose. "Our director's really going for it."

Kumiko personally thought he was pretty full of himself but kept quiet.

"In any case, for today's ensemble practice I'd like to focus on the places where the mistakes were the most obvious. So, let's begin from the trumpet melody in the middle…"

At Taki's signal, the band readied their instruments. Among them, of course, was Reina. She looked straight at Taki, and although Kumiko couldn't see her eyes, she could tell his expression was perfectly reflected in Reina's serious features.

After that fateful ensemble practice, the sounds of sectionals became much more prominent all over the school. Kumiko wondered if the students who'd been ditching had started attending again. She didn't know how much of it was thanks to Taki's instruction, but she knew for sure that some of the students newly applying themselves to practice were doing so out of spite. During trips to the girls' bathroom next to the music classroom she heard plenty of muttering about "that asshole teacher" or "the sneaky bastard," but—they could complain as much as they liked as long as they came to practice.

"Wait, no, I don't get it."

When Kumiko arrived at the day's sectionals, she found Hazuki looking up to Takuya in confusion. He was pointing at the sheet music and scratching his head, clearly at a loss.

"Like...you just have to use your throat and tongue...I think. Probably."

"No way. That's impossible."

"You can do it. It'll be fine."

"Uh-uh. This is just too hard."

Kumiko peered over at what the two were discussing. It was the practice regimen that Taki had devised. It came with sheet music that had been numbered—#1, #2, and so on—which was probably for fundamental skills practice.

The most important skill for a brass instrument was the long tone. Playing the notes of the scale was a basic technique, but practicing long tones helped stabilize the player's sound. The more time spent practicing conscious control of the breath that produced the sound, the more beautiful the sound would become. Taki put great stock in long tones, and he had handed out quite a bit of sheet music on the subject that was meant solely for practice.

Hazuki was currently engaged in a furious struggle with lip slurs, which were an especially important technique for instruments that could produce different notes with a single fingering. The exercise consisted of playing different pitches without moving the pistons. The key to this was trying to change the sound not with the lips but rather by controlling the muscles of the mouth and the speed of the breath simultaneously. Hazuki, having just started with her instrument, seemed to find this too difficult, wincing and groaning at the prospect.

"Hmm. I don't know anything about brass!" said Midori, sounding weirdly proud as she looked at the sheet music in question. With no other contrabass players in the band, Midori had no seniors to instruct her. Nonetheless, she was a force to be reckoned with, readily able to play the parts asked of her. Her middle school was known for its music program, after all.

"What're you grumbling about? Forget about playing it on the horn—you gotta master it on the mouthpiece by itself, first!"

Of course it was Asuka who burst in on the conversation. She was supposed to still be in the middle of a career guidance counseling appointment, but here she was, standing next to Hazuki and brimming with enthusiasm to play.

Takuya made a long-suffering face. "Tanaka, what about your guidance counseling?"

"I wrapped that bad boy up in five minutes! Career guidance? I'd like to see someone try to *stop* my career!"

Takuya sighed in capitulation, apparently lacking the energy for a comeback. "…Okay."

"So, Hazuki! Having trouble with your lip slurs?"

"Er, yes," nodded Hazuki, overawed.

"I'll show you how I do it. Put your horn down and try just blowing through the mouthpiece."

Hazuki did as Asuka instructed and set her tuba down on the floor. Like other brass instruments in the bass section, the proper way to stand the tuba up was on its bell. Hazuki's instrument was battered and worn, with its shiny plating flaking off here and there. The sheer size of a tuba meant it was expensive, and given that several of its smaller cousins could be purchased for the same cost of just one new tuba, replacing them tended to be put off.

"Now, first. Can you make a sound with just the mouthpiece?"

"Um, yes. Like this?" Hazuki pressed her lips together, and held against the opening of the small metal component, they produced a rather unbeautiful buzzing sound.

Asuka nodded, satisfied. "That's the way." She then brought her own mouthpiece to her lips. "Now, try changing the pitch. Like this." Asuka demonstrated shifting the note that was coming out of the mouthpiece. The change in sound was so obvious that Kumiko was surprised. She'd never known that you could get such clearly defined tones out of just a mouthpiece.

"The problem is it's hard even before I get that far," said Hazuki, her eyebrows drooping in consternation.

Asuka continued her instruction, but Kumiko couldn't restrain her curiosity. She furtively put her own mouthpiece to her lips, trying to avoid anyone noticing.

"…"

She did manage to play some notes, but she was far from Asuka's skill. For one thing, her tone wasn't nearly as clean. Maybe there was a problem with her breathing. Unlike Asuka's long, steady sound, Kumiko's tended to waver and drift flat. She wondered what she would have to do to sound as beautiful as Asuka did.

"You're pretty good."

"Wyaah!" Kumiko shouted in surprise at the voice behind her. She looked over her shoulder to see the deadpan Takuya peering at her.

"Nakagawa can't do that at all."

"You mean Natsuki?"

"Right. She can't blow without the horn on."

"Oh, I see."

"I mean, I'm not as good as Tanaka is, either, but still," said Takuya, hunching his huge body over.

"So, Gotou—when did you start playing the tuba?"

"What, me?" He pointed to himself and tilted his head.

"Natsuki and Riko started in high school, right? So when did you start playing in a band?"

Takuya folded his arms as though thinking it over, eventually murmuring an answer. "I guess…the winter of my first year in middle school, maybe. I quit track and joined the concert band."

"You did track?"

"Yeah. But ever since then it's been all tuba."

"You haven't gotten bored with always playing the same instrument?"

"I do not," Takuya answered immediately. "I like the tuba."

He looked down, perhaps embarrassed by his own words. A faint crimson flush rose to his round cheeks. His face in profile was somehow so resplendent that Kumiko couldn't help but look away.

The month of April seemed to evaporate in the repetition of ensemble practice, then sectionals, then ensemble, then sectionals.

Kumiko looked down at her day planner with exhaustion on her face. The SunFest was next week. After much thought, she realized it would be her first performance as a high school student. And right after that would be her first midterms as a high school student. Imagining the number of practice questions she'd face beforehand did not improve her mood.

"Okay, we're going to distribute the uniforms we'll be wearing for next week's performance."

At the sound of Ogasawara's voice, Kumiko drew a sharp breath and looked up. The clock's hands were both pointing straight up at the 12. Noon brought with it their outdoor practice in the courtyard, which made Kumiko's gloom even heavier. The prospect of practicing under direct sunlight was not an appealing one.

"First-year students, please make sure to come and get yours. Now, starting with percussion…"

At the front of the classroom, Asuka took bags out of a cardboard box. Probably the marching uniforms, Kumiko guessed. They'd taken all the first-year students' measurements a week earlier, which Kumiko just now realized must have been for this.

"Pretty exciting, right?" Hazuki was seated next to Kumiko, and her eyes shone.

Next to Hazuki was Midori, murmuring grimly. "What if they're gross? I swear I'll die if they make me wear something lame."

Kumiko had never heard Midori sound so serious about anything. Evidently she cared more about fashion than the average person—in which regard she couldn't have been more different from Kumiko, who would wear anything that fit.

"Next! Bass section!"

"Ah, coming!" The three girls hastily stood at Asuka's call. The plastic bags they received were much heavier than Kumiko had expected.

"A jacket, huh? That's gonna get hot!" cried Hazuki upon ripping her bag open. Next to her, Midori carefully cut her bag open with a pair of scissors. For Kumiko's part, she felt for the bag's small opening, then forced it wider with her fingers. From within the bag she produced a black dress shirt, black pants, a blue jacket, and a black fedora with a blue ribbon.

"We'll start midday practice once everybody's changed, since this is a rehearsal. Anybody whose uniform doesn't fit, make sure to let me know."

The president was met with a listless, albeit affirmative, response. Midori stared at the outfit for a while. "...Oh well, could've been worse!" she finally murmured.

"We'll use this room for the girls, and Class Three's room next door for the boys, so everybody hurry and get changed, then bring your instruments down and assemble in front of the big pine tree in the courtyard."

"Okay!" The band confirmed Asuka's instructions, and then there was chaos. The boys practically fled the room, and once they were gone the girls began to take off their sailor-suit uniforms without any particular shyness. Kumiko caught herself looking away from the seniors as they strode around in their underwear.

She tried on the outfit. The sizing seemed just about perfect, since it felt completely familiar even though she was wearing it for the first time. The stripes that ran down the sides of the pants were decorated in blue sequins that sparkled with Kumiko's every move. The shoes they would wear in the performances matched, as well—simple black sneakers with blue lines.

"Whaddaya think? Look good?" Hazuki said with a smug look on her face as she approached Kumiko. The uniform did indeed look very good on an athletic girl like Hazuki.

"You're so lucky. I wish I could march with my bass," muttered Midori, standing next to Hazuki and trying on the hat.

"Yeah, I don't think that's gonna happen."

"I know, I know," said Midori, pouting. Since the contrabass was not an instrument that could be played while marching, Midori wouldn't be performing. Evidently she would be walking ahead of the band along with the beginners, waving to the spectators.

"Kumiko, make sure you put on sunscreen, okay?" The voice was Aoi's, calling out to Kumiko from behind her. With the saxophone hanging from her neck, she looked quite put together.

"Oh, you think I'll burn?"

"You definitely will. And just your face, too."

"Ugh, nooo."

"Then be careful. The long sleeves will keep your arms from burning, at least." Aoi smiled pleasantly, but then from behind her a girl's voice rose in a shrill cry.

"Eeeee! Kaori, you look adorable! You're seriously, like, an angel!"

Everyone's gaze turned to the source of the sound. It was a second-year trumpet player named Yuuko Yoshikawa, breathing raggedly through her nose and clenching her fist with conviction. Her eyes, meanwhile, were fixed intently on Kaori.

"R-really?" A flush came to Kaori's cheeks. And indeed there was something angelic about the loveliness of her shyly upturned gaze as she looked back to Yuuko.

Then—the already-changed Asuka jumped in. "Whoa, that's Kaori for ya! So cute!"

The bass section's fearless leader, with her outstanding proportions, was the absolute opposite of "cute." Her long black hair was tied up in a high ponytail, taking her well past anything resembling feminine allure and straight into handsome territory. Her gallant figure seemed particularly effective on the more boy-crazy girls, and some of the poor first-years staggered as they whimpered, "Hold me!" or "I could just die!" Asuka and Kaori did indeed make a lovely picture, standing together like that.

"You look awesome, too, Asuka."

"Heh-heh. Thanks." Asuka flashed her signature grin at the blushing Kaori's compliment.

Kaori gently reached out and pulled on the other girl's arm. Her jacket wrinkled with the motion.

Asuka's sharp profile turned toward Kaori. "...What's up?" She tilted her head curiously.

Kaori's eyes widened at this, and she reddened still further, hastily letting go of Asuka's arm. "N-nothing, never mind!"

"Okay," said Asuka. A faint smile played at the corners of her mouth as she patted Kaori on the shoulder before looking over the rest of the classroom. "All right! Everybody who's changed, let's get moving!"

At Asuka's direction, everyone hastily started getting ready to leave. For a moment, Kaori looked at Asuka as though she wanted to say something, but in the end her lips were unable to form the words.

"Ugh, so heavy..."

Riko was usually gentle and sweet, but the sun had even her grimacing. Around her coiled that famous marching instrument, the sousaphone. The tuba she normally played was too heavy for a parade, and it was for that exact purpose that the sousaphone had been created. Kitauji's sousaphones were made mostly of fiberglass, and more of their weight was distributed over the players' shoulders, making them easier to carry. However, they still weighed ten kilograms each, which was more than enough for them to feel awfully heavy in the students' arms while they played.

"Oh man, so I'm gonna have to wear one of those when I march..." said a pale-faced Hazuki, next to Riko.

Next to Hazuki was Midori, who was happily waving a red-and-blue flag. Band members like her, who marched with flags, were called the color guard.

"I haven't done guard for a while. Hope I'll do okay."

"Wait, don't you just have to, like, wave?" asked Kumiko.

"That's what I asked," said Midori, looking worried. "But then I got asked to do more. I guess it's just going to be me and one of the flute seniors, so hopefully it won't be too hard to get in sync."

"Midori, you can do color guard? You're really handy!" said Riko, impressed.

"For real, she can do anything," added Hazuki.

"Aww, you guys!" giggled Midori, pleased.

Natsuki approached her from behind, hanging a languid arm over her shoulders. "So, did you master the mystery step?"

"Th-the mystery step? Oh, you said something about that before, too," said Kumiko, to which Natsuki nodded.

"That's right. Kitauji High School's famous mystery step! It's tradition for first-year beginners to perform it at the SunFest."

"Sounds tough."

Since Kumiko had experience on her instrument, she had nothing to do with this "mystery step" business. During the actual performance, all she would have to do was walk and play her instrument. Natsuki, meanwhile, enthusiastically launched into her explanation of this year's marching formation.

"So since all the conducting has to happen while we're walking, Mr. Taki won't be conducting us. The drum major will be marching at the front. That'll be Asuka."

"What's a drum major do?" asked Hazuki.

"They're like the conductor for a marching band. They're like the face of our band, leading us and waving their baton around."

The drum major often acted as the coordinator for the band as a whole, giving them direction when it was required. It would be ideal to choose someone popular, with both technical proficiency and excellent interpersonal skills. On those counts, there were no problems with Asuka at all. No problems at all. But.

"...So President Ogasawara isn't going to be the drum major?"

Riko's expression clouded at Kumiko's question. "Ogasawara doesn't really have the right mind-set. She's not really cut out for it."

"But she still became the club president?" said Hazuki curiously.

Riko scratched her head nervously. "Yeah. I mean, really everybody wanted Asuka to be president, but apparently Asuka hates stuff like that. She didn't even really want to be vice president, but after we begged her she finally gave in."

"I dunno about that," said Midori. "Asuka seems super leader-y to me."

Kumiko nodded at Midori's words. Asuka was definitely the type of person who wound up in charge.

But Natsuki snickered as though she had read Kumiko's mind. "But being good at something and being interested in doing it are two different things, aren't they? And Ogasawara's doing a good job as president. Kinda feel bad for her always being compared to Asuka," she said, sighing bodily. She pushed her short, neatly trimmed hair back behind her ear and continued her explanation.

"So first come the two guards. Then the drum major. Then after a little gap comes the brass. And by the way, the trombones march in front! Anybody in front of them would get their head knocked by those slides. Then between the brass and the woodwinds are the battery—the percussion section. See the guys with the drums hanging off 'em? When people say 'the battery,' that's who they're talking about," said Natsuki, pointing to the percussion section as they practiced. They were carrying snare drums and bass drums, and receiving instruction from the seniors on how to play while marching.

"The first-year beginners follow behind the woodwinds. They wave around pom-poms—you know, like the cheerleading club has—and perform the mystery step."

After all that, despite the explanation, the nature of the mystery step was still entirely mysterious. Midori had lost interest halfway through and was now happily waving her color guard flag around. Natsuki suddenly heaved a deep sigh, her arm still hanging around Hazuki, She was looking at the second-year student from earlier—Yuuko. Yuuko, meanwhile, circled around Kaori like a small, adoring dog.

"Yuuko sure does love Kaori," murmured Hazuki, prompting a meaningful grin in agreement from Natsuki.

"Okay, time for practice!" announced Asuka.

Everyone stood. As soon as they stepped out from beneath the shade of the tree, they were in full sunlight. Patches of brilliance skittered here and there from the light reflecting off the glittering instruments. There were close to eighty students in the courtyard, and seeing them all together outside like this made the size of the band very clear.

"We'll start with step practice for the first-years. Everybody stepping, line up!"

At these instructions, the first-year beginners all filtered to the center of the yard in a line. There were twenty-eight new first-year students, but only ten lacked previous instrument experience.

"The step is just like how I explained earlier—right, front, return; then left, front, return; then repeat. Your hands alternate—first up, then down."

"Yes, ma'am!" replied the first-years to Ogasawara's instructions.

Asuka clapped her hands together twice. "All right, we'll start marching practice from here! At the event we'll be doing one lap around Taiyou Park, so it'll be about one kilometer. It'll be rough, but keep that smile going!"

"Yes, ma'am!"

"Okay, line up!"

At Asuka's words, the band naturally lined up into formation. Kumiko stood next to Natsuki. Without Asuka, they were down to two euphoniums. Behind them were Takuya and Riko—evidently the large bells of their sousaphones would get in the way otherwise.

"First we'll do circuits around the courtyard." Asuka stood at a short remove and began to clap her hands. "Five, six, seven, eight..."

At these words, the entire band brought their right legs up, knees high, then began to march to the percussion section's rhythm. The front ranks and the rear advanced, the band members taking care not to slip out of formation. Walking while playing wind and brass instruments made the mouthpieces jiggle up and down, which caused the sound to fluctuate. Actually doing it made it obvious how different playing while marching was from playing in a sitting position. Unlike in ensemble practice, the smallest trigger could wreck the music. Since sound had to travel through the air, the front ranks and rear ranks heard slightly different rhythms from the drums between them. Preventing those differences from turning into mistakes was the drum major's job, but it was hard for Kumiko to keep her eyes on Asuka when she was so focused on moving her legs correctly. Her left hand, which supported the weight of her euphonium, was starting to tremble from the effort.

"Today's all about walking! Don't stop moving your feet!" Asuka barked.

Kumiko gave a desperate, silent howl.

*   *   *

Kumiko regarded the pamphlet for the Twenty-Third Annual Sunrise Festival and let loose a great sigh. Sitting in the bus, she caught snippets of her classmates' conversations here and there.

"Whoa! Did you see that? A four-leaf clover taxi just went zooming by!" An excited Midori, staring intently out the bus's window, tugged on Kumiko's shirt. Was Midori really even a high school student? Kumiko felt like a kindergarten teacher as she answered with a patronizing *good-for-you!* smile. Midori seemed satisfied by the response, since she let go of Kumiko's shirt and returned to gazing out the window.

The SunFest began at nine AM, so the band's arrival and assembly schedule was quite early. The park and the school itself were not very far removed from each other, so the actual transit time wasn't too long. Since the percussion, tubas, and other large instruments had been trucked over the night before, there wasn't too much left to do the day of the event. But between changing into her marching uniform, getting her hair ready, and reviewing the marching formation, the time vanished quickly anyway.

"Okay, guys, hurry up and get on the bus!"

Everyone followed the president's instructions. Seating inside the bus was a free-for-all, and there was a considerable amount of bargaining to be done before it was settled. Cliques with an odd number of members would obviously not fit neatly into the bus's two-seat sections, so everyone was vaguely trying to find a partner to pair up with. Leftover students tried to appear unconcerned as they furtively glanced around in a hasty attempt to avoid being branded a sad loner. The mundane churn of the students concealed countless tiny dramas—here, someone saw the friend they'd planned to sit with sit next to someone else. There, a carefully planned, even-numbered group was scattered by seating availability. It was in times like these that Kumiko found it dreadfully tiresome to have to be a high school student all the time.

"Let's all do our best today," Taki said, speaking up as soon as he boarded the bus. His tone of voice made it seem like he was talking about something that had nothing to do with him at all, and he wore the same pleasant smile he always did. Next to him stood a sleepy Michie, her arms crossed.

"Hey, Kumiko! Have you ever listened to 'Can't Buy Me Love'? The original Beatles one, not the band arrangement we do," asked Midori. Apparently bored with staring out the window, she tugged on Kumiko's arm.

Lost in her rumination, Kumiko didn't immediately move her head to react to the question. She finally responded to the question with a quiet "Huh?"

"The Beatles version! Like I was saying!"

"Um, no, I don't know it."

"How can you not? It's so cool! I *adore* the Beatles. 'Cause my dad loves 'em."

"Ah, okay."

"You should really give 'em a listen, Kumiko! 'Cause they're so cool," Midori said, then started humming her part from the song.

"Well, let's play it together at the competition," replied Kumiko.

Midori's only answer was to intensify her smile as she continued to hum. Her voice flowed into the chatter that suffused the bus's interior, but the tenuous, lovely little melody never reached anyone's ears before it dissolved into the din.

The students exited the bus into a great crowd made of participants and spectators alike. Kumiko and the rest of the uniform-clad band hurried to the truck where their instruments awaited. Bands from other schools were already warming up on the park's green lawn. She heard long tones sounding from here and there and wondered if they were tuning.

"Okay, people! Get the percussion unloaded first—trumpets, clarinets, and anything else you can carry yourself can wait. Don't start setting up until all the instruments are unloaded!"

Following Asuka's directions, the students rapidly began to take the instruments from the truck. Kumiko pointlessly wondered why the sousaphone was so strangely shaped as she tried a variety of different approaches to carrying it.

Once the instruments were unloaded, the band swiftly set about making ready, with everyone opening their own cases and putting together their instruments. Midori carried her flag over to the senior band member responsible for the color guard and consulted her about something. Hazuki held her pom-poms and practiced her steps. And with nothing else to do, Kumiko held her euphonium and exhaled a short sigh.

"We've got this!" said Riko as she approached Kumiko. From her face, she looked like she was already beat. The giant sousaphone might have been exhausting to carry, but it was exciting to see. The giant, pure-white bell made a pleasing contrast with their dark blue uniforms.

Natsuki approached, carrying her euphonium and holding out a small pink tuner. "You better tune up, or you're gonna run out of time. Here, you can use mine."

Kumiko hastily readied her instrument. Natsuki frowned as she indicated pitch adjustments sharp or flat. Kumiko pushed and pulled the tuning tube accordingly, eventually arriving at a stable, correct note.

"Rikka's gonna be here soon, so we gotta wrap up and be ready to hand over the space."

"Rikka High School..." Kumiko murmured.

There wasn't a concert band student in Kyoto who didn't know about Rikka High School. It was an elite private school that boasted a lengthy and impressive record in band competitions and marching festivals. They were often on television, so even people without much interest in concert bands knew the school's name.

"Did you hear they call 'em 'the powder-blue devils'?"

"The powder-blue devils?" It was an unsettling name for an all-girl group.

Riko nodded. "That's right. They go jumping and dancing all over the place with these crazy smiles. You should definitely see them sometime. It'll make you realize what it takes to compete at the national level."

"I swear they're demons wearing human skin. I'm barely even joking," said Natsuki. It was rare for her to get so worked up.

Kumiko had seen Rikka a few times on TV but never in person. If she was lucky, today might be the day she got to hear them perform. The day's potential outcome had improved by one good thing, Kumiko mused, but just then a high, beautiful tone from a trumpet interrupted her thoughts, piercing through the chatter around her. There was no mistaking it—it was the sound of Reina tuning. Realizing as much, Kumiko stopped short—why was Reina's sound so clear? There had been quite a tumult surrounding Kumiko, after all.

The answer arrived surprisingly quickly. Everyone else had stopped playing. Even students from other schools were looking at Reina, and an odd silence had fallen. The girl in question either did not notice or was pretending not to with a completely unconcerned expression, as she played another tone on her trumpet.

"Who's that girl? She's good."

"What school's she with?"

"That blue jacket...that's Kitauji, right?"

"Huh? What's someone as good as her going there for? What a waste."

"Waste is right."

"She could've at least picked a school that would've actually used her."

The whispers of students from other schools were audible even from where Kumiko was. Reina's expression was unmoved as she continued to play her long tones. Some of the third-year students watching her seemed to be getting irritated.

Kumiko glanced over at Ogasawara, who was hastily turning her head this way and that as though at a loss over what to do about the situation. Finally, Asuka clapped her hands twice—it seemed like she couldn't stand to watch the situation play out any further.

"Okay, attention, everybody! We're gonna be moving out soon!"

"Okay!" came the band's reply as they sprang into a flurry of brisk movement. Asuka had completely dispelled the momentary awkwardness. She really was a superb manipulator of mood.

"I'm sorry I'm so useless, Asuka," whispered Ogasawara into the vice president's ear. Ogasawara normally stood up straight, but now she hunched over gloomily.

The ever-reliable vice president flashed a white-toothed grin. "What're you talking about? I didn't do anything."

"But, I mean…"

"Who cares about these silly little details, anyway? You should be thinking about today's main event!" Asuka chuckled and slapped Ogasawara on the back.

A junior band student approached. "Um, Asuka, about the formation today…"

"Hm? Sure, I'll be right there. Okay, Haruka—later!" said Asuka before trotting jauntily away. As she receded, her uniformed figure was as reliable as ever. Ogasawara watched her go and finally heaved a big sigh. "…At this rate, I'm not even sure who's the president anymore," she murmured.

Her voice was small and thin, with interweaving threads of self-mockery and impatience. As Kumiko looked on, Haruka—though she was two years older than Kumiko—almost sounded ready to cry.

"I'm very much looking forward to your performance."

"And you won't get away with slacking off!"

With these comforting, kind words from its director and assistant director, the Kitauji High School Concert Band formed up to march to their assigned place. This year's SunFest featured sixteen ensembles. At fixed intervals, each of them would begin to march along the parade's route. Kitauji was fifth from the front, and Rikka would be marching last. Depending on when Kitauji finished, if they hurried, they might be able to catch Rikka's performance.

"I'm kinda…more nervous than usual, today," said Takuya as he lined up behind Kumiko. His expression was certainly tenser than usual.

Natsuki cackled. "Well, that's what we get for practicing so hard."

"Yeah. I mean, this is the hardest any of us have practiced since joining the band," said Riko with an emphatic nod. And it was true—the amount of practice had been truly stupendous. And while the schedule Taki had distributed was bad enough, most of the psychological impact had come during the ensemble practices.

"He's just such a stickler," said Kumiko quietly.

Takuya nodded in emphatic agreement. "It was rough."

"Making us play stuff a million times, over and over again! And don't you think he's crazy about tuning? Like, being so picky when you can't even hear the difference…" said Natsuki.

"Yeah, I would never have guessed Mr. Taki would be that type. Our director last year was so much nicer…" said Riko with nostalgia in her voice.

"Whoops, we're gonna start." Natsuki's words brought everyone out of their reveries. Asuka raised her drum major's baton. At her whistle, the drums began to sound their rhythm, and the performance commenced. Kumiko began to march, leading with her right foot as she kept the formation in her mind.

Parades were fun—physically demanding, but fun. Kumiko marched in her rank, moving her body to the rhythm. Taki's instruction had been intense, but not for nothing; the students could feel the difference. Their once-messy playing was now synchronized, each instrument sounding out properly. Drilling the fundamentals seemed to have stabilized their tone. Taki's fixation on details had made all of them that much better. He was an excellent teacher—which was why his inability to recognize their increasing skill was so frustrating.

"They look great!"

"Dang, Kitauji's pretty good."

"That girl at the front's a hottie!"

"Was this school always this good?"

As she heard the voices of the onlookers, something hot began to overflow from inside her mind, melting Kumiko's tension away. The heat carried her thoughts to a place far, far away from reason. Although her feet were leaden and heavy, her spirits weren't the least bit dampened. She felt like she could march forever.

The music didn't stop. When they reached the end of the score, the band returned to the beginning. Over and over they repeated it.

She didn't have to think about the sheet music. Her body remembered it. She heard the sunny cheers coming from behind her, surely directed at the energetic performance of the snare drums. Their complex rhythms were in perfect sync, not even a millisecond off. When the percussion section finished, they waved and received warm applause in response. Then the trumpet melody sounded, followed by the bass section—the latter never stood out, though. That was fine with Kumiko. That was the fun part of playing in the bass section. Kumiko spurned the part of her that quavered from exhaustion and summoned what remained of her strength. She'd lost feeling in her left hand from supporting her euphonium. And still, she didn't want to stop—it was too much fun!

A mysterious elation controlled Kumiko's body, though she didn't clearly remember how she had come this far. Finally the end of the parade route came into view. Asuka's drum major baton thrust high into the air. Forcing her exhausted legs on, her thighs burning each time she raised a knee, Kumiko somehow managed to finish.

Their performance over, the band members hurried to put away their instruments—if they lingered too long at the finishing area, they'd be in the way of the bands coming behind them. Taki calmly addressed the sweaty, ragged group.

"Now that you've finished putting away your instruments, you're free until three o'clock. Feel free to take a break, but considering the summer competition, I suggest going to listen to the other bands' performances. In particular, Rikka High School won a gold medal at last year's national competition, so I strongly recommend seeing them play."

It was Midori who reacted the most strongly to Taki's advice. "Kumiko, quick, hurry! We gotta go see Rikka play!" She tugged on Kumiko's and Hazuki's arms, her eyes sparkling.

"C'mon, we don't hafta hurry *that* much..." moaned a ragged Hazuki.

"Yes we do!" objected Midori, her cheeks puffing out like a

stubborn squirrel's. "We've *got* to see them! I've been looking forward to it all day! It's what got me through!"

"Really?"

"Yes!"

There was nothing to do in the face of such strength. Kumiko and Hazuki let Midori drag them in search of a place to watch from. There were obviously more spectators now than there had been when Kitauji had passed along the route, and it was clear that Rikka was the main event.

"We should be able to see them soon!" said Midori, delighted. Despite running around here and there all along the route, the girl seemed to have a bottomless well of stamina. Turning away from the dazed Hazuki, Kumiko directed her attention toward the parade.

"There they are!" cried Midori.

From across the way, the pale blue band approached. Despite that considerable distance, their sound was already very clear. The flawless tones that issued from their instruments pierced the air and resounded cleanly in Kumiko's ears. The lively, simple sounds landed amid the cheers of the crowd.

"'Anchors Aweigh'! Cool!" said Midori. The familiar music was a march that had been composed by Charles Zimmerman in 1906, when he was a lieutenant in the United States Navy.

Rikka High School's marching band uniforms were extremely cute. The smart, crisp powder-blue dresses stood out pleasantly against the park lawn's green. The finish line was not far away. Despite having marched for nearly a kilometer, the band's members smiled proudly as they went. They didn't look remotely tired. Kumiko suddenly understood why people called them "the powder-blue devils." They practically danced as they played—the woodwinds springing up and down and the brass swinging their bells side to side as they marched. The most terrifying part was that despite their exaggerated movements, their performance was rock-solid. How much did you have to practice to be good enough to pull that off? Kumiko wondered if there was some kind of secret to it, as she stared at the faces in the band.

"Hm?" Suddenly she met the eyes of a particular member. "Wait, that's Azusa."

Azusa had been a classmate of Kumiko's in middle school. She'd played trombone at the time, and evidently still did, for that was the instrument on which she was performing at that very moment.

"You know her?" Midori asked.

Kumiko nodded and waved to the Rikka High School band. Azusa's eyes squinted, and she swung her instrument happily. Kumiko wasn't sure, but she thought Azusa had noticed.

"Still, I was really surprised! Never thought we'd run into each other like that," said Azusa.

After the SunFest had ended and the bands had been dismissed, Kumiko had met up with Azusa. When the two had been friends in middle school, they'd often used the JR Uji Station as a meeting spot. The station had been designed to evoke the ancient Phoenix Hall of Byoudou-in, and Azusa was terribly fond of it, stopping to take snapshots of it with her cell phone at every opportunity. There was a giant tea jar at the station's south entrance—it was actually a specially made mailbox—and this, too, was a favorite of Azusa's. She always stopped to take a picture.

"Still, I had no idea you were going to Rikka."

"That's right. I went for the band. They're total diehards, though." Azusa grinned over the matcha soft-serve ice cream cone she'd bought at a tea shop.

Kumiko returned the smile, then glanced down at her own roasted tea-flavored cone of soft serve. She wondered if she should've gone with matcha. Even in times like these, her chronic indecisiveness showed its face.

"But Kitauji's gotten way better, too. They're totally different from last year."

"Probably 'cause we have a new director."

"Seriously, you guys have gotten really good. On the bus everyone was like, 'a new challenger appears'!"

"Rikka was really good, too."

"I guess, but, you know—of course we were. It's Rikka," said Azusa, straightening proudly. Her unabashed pride in her school was backed up with effort and results, though, which Kumiko envied a bit. Kumiko looked away and licked her ice cream.

The two were quiet, and for a while they wordlessly walked along the riverbank. The evening sun sank lower, its redly ripened circle melting down between the buildings of the city. A lingering shade of red tinged the edges of the indigo sky. The white moon rose hesitantly, the announcement of night's arrival.

"Hey, Kumiko. Why didn't you go to Minamiuji High School?" asked Azusa.

The question was so sudden that it took Kumiko a moment to realize what it actually meant. "Why would you expect me to have gone there?"

"I mean, most of the students from Kitachu wound up at Minamiuji, so I figured that was where you'd gone, too." Azusa stopped walking. A drop of her melting ice cream fell on the grass at their feet.

Kumiko smiled. "There's lots of reasons to pick a school. Academics, or distance, say."

"Sure, but Minamiuji's closer, and their grades are about the same."

"That's true, but…"

Pressed on her reasoning, Kumiko fell silent. Azusa waited for a proper reply.

"I guess there wasn't a specific reason, but…" Kumiko began. "…I wanted a reset."

"A reset?" Azusa tilted her head. The river glittered under the city's evening lights. The water's surface was beautiful, but Kumiko had no notion of what was beneath it. What might be lurking in that night-colored water? She couldn't know.

"I just wanted to start over. I wanted to go to a school where I didn't know too many people. So that's why I went to Kitauji. That's all."

Kumiko smiled. She didn't much like putting her own thoughts into words. It hurt too much when they were criticized.

Azusa nodded thoughtfully. "I see," she said with a smile, and for some reason she looked incredibly relieved.

A trace of childishness remained in the soft lines of Azusa's features. Kumiko's gaze wandered down along her neck to where her collarbones peeked out from behind her shirt, the swell of her chest distinct through the fabric. Though a certain girlishness remained, Azusa was steadily moving toward adulthood. Leaving Kumiko behind.

"So you really thought it over, then," said Azusa.

"Thought what over?"

"Sorry, sorry—I just figured when you picked schools, someone had pushed you to just go with the flow again." Azusa smiled a pleasant smile. She popped the last bit of what remained of her ice cream cone into her mouth, then stretched. "The next time we see each other will probably be the competition."

"Probably."

"We couldn't pull it off in middle school, but...for high school, I really want to make it to Nationals."

"Yeah." Kumiko smiled softly. She didn't really think she'd be able to go, but it would be awfully nice. "You'll definitely make it, Azusa. I mean, it's Rikka."

"Yeah, probably." The corner of Azusa's mouth curled in a fearless smile, but then her expression quickly changed. Her fine eyelashes fluttered, and she seemed to remember something. "Oh, wait—didn't Reina end up going to your school?"

"Yeah, why?"

"Why'd *she* go to Kitauji?"

Ugh, this again? Kumiko thought to herself, her brows furrowing as she remembered what had happened earlier. Sure, Reina was a talented player, and sure, maybe her ability was kind of wasted on the Kitauji Concert Band—but you didn't have to come right out and say it like that.

Azusa seemed to notice Kumiko's displeasure and hastily shook her head. "No, no, I mean—I know she was offered a full scholarship to Rikka, is all."

"Yeah, she's really smart..."

"And I'm sure she had a recommendation for the band, too, but for whatever reason, even though she was admitted, I never saw her. I always thought it was strange, but I never guessed she was at Kitauji," said Azusa, confusion on her face. "Why didn't she come to Rikka? If she's really serious about band, we'd definitely have been the best choice."

"That's true..." Kumiko was just as puzzled. The more she learned about Reina, the more mysteries there were. What had she been thinking when she'd decided on Kitauji High School?

"Anyway. Let's both practice hard!" said Azusa, waving.

Kumiko returned the wave. This classmate she hadn't seen in quite a while seemed, somehow, just a bit more grown-up.

3 ♪ Welcome Back, Audition ♪

With the end of Golden Week, studies began in earnest for the bulk of Kitauji's students. The week before the midterm exams, all extracurricular activities were canceled. Pushing her normally recalcitrant brain to full throttle, Kumiko managed to get through the tests. Her scores were slightly above the average. Not bad—although not good, either.

"Congratulations on finishing your midterm exams."

It was the first day off school since the tests were over. The assembled members of the band all gazed meekly at Taki's face. Their own expressions were, to a one, suffused with an obvious unease.

"Now then, with midterms out of the way, the only big event between now and the summer break will be your finals."

Kumiko involuntarily winced. She wished he wouldn't count finals as a "big event." Just thinking about them dampened her already-gloomy spirits.

"The concert band has nothing scheduled until we appear in competition, so you should all have plenty of time to practice."

Kumiko had a bad feeling about this. And just as she'd feared, Taki pulled a slip of paper out of his pocket.

"This paper contains this year's list of compulsory pieces."

"Compulsory...pieces?"

For Class A and Full Band competitions (including Nationals), competitors were required to perform both a compulsory piece and a free piece. For the compulsory piece, participating bands chose whichever one they preferred from the provided list of options and performed it at the competition. There were also limitations on the size of the ensemble, with high school bands capped at fifty-five members. The performance time, too, was limited—the compulsory and free performances combined had to be less than twelve minutes. Exceeding twelve minutes resulted in immediate disqualification. There were no exceptions to this twelve-minute rule, and disqualifications for violating it were not uncommon even at Nationals. It was a surprisingly strict form of competition.

"I don't know how you've chosen your performance pieces in the past, but this year Ms. Matsumoto and I will be making the decision for both the compulsory and free performances. I apologize to anyone who had expectations otherwise." Taki did not seem notably apologetic.

"So, what will this year's songs be?" Asuka's eyes shone.

Taki made a deliberate show of holding his mouth closed for a moment, then suddenly exhaled. "Our compulsory piece this year will be Namie Horikawa's 'Crescent Moon Dance,' and our free will be 'East Coast Pictures.'"

That was all well and good, but Kumiko had no idea what kind of music either of those pieces was. Evidently she wasn't the only one, as the students' applause upon hearing the titles was distinctly hesitant and uncertain.

"'Crescent Moon Dance'! Mr. Taki, you really know what's what, don't you?" Asuka shot to her feet, her cheeks colored with her excitement. She appeared to be the only student in the room who had any familiarity with the music in question. "Namie Horikawa! She's a young composer born in Kyoto who got her MFA in composition at the Kyoto City University of Arts! A woman whose zeitgeist-capturing work ranges from orchestral compositions to wind ensembles, and her appeal comes from her intricate melodies and dynamic structure! Her bass harmonies are supercool, too. I just *knew* we had to play 'Crescent Moon Dance'! And—"

"I'm glad you're happy with our choices, Miss Tanaka," said Taki, mercilessly cutting Asuka off. Though her enthusiasm wasn't dampened in the slightest, she sat, clasping her hands together in joy and continuing to regale Kaori, who sat next to her.

"Now then, I have something important to discuss," continued Taki, eyes scanning over the assembled band. "There are eighty-one students in the concert band this year. Ten of those are beginners, but that still leaves seventy-one students who can perform in Class A. However, Class A competition limits ensembles to fifty-five members. We simply have too many."

Everyone held their breath. Only fifty-five students would be able to play in Class A competitions. Obviously, some eligible students would be left out.

Taki smiled and continued. "Therefore, I have decided to hold auditions over the two days leading up to your final exams."

Auditions. The third-year students were the first to react. Ignoring the excited murmurs of the first-year students, the third-year girls stood and immediately began arguing with Taki.

"Mr. Taki, we've always decided competition band lineup by school year. Shouldn't first-year students play in Class B, instead?"

Class A wasn't the only category in concert band competition. At the local and regional levels, there were elementary school categories and small-ensemble categories, which were known as Class B, and events involving the combined class, Class C, were also common. They didn't lead to the national competition, but they were a way for bands with constraints on their membership or budget to participate in smaller competitions. It was common for schools with larger bands to participate in both Class A and Class B, and Kitauji had always done so.

"Isn't that unfair, though?" Taki's smile was undamaged. "Many of the first-year students are working just as hard. It strikes me as unreasonable to ignore their effort and decide band lineup by class year."

"But that's what we've always done."

"Yes, but I'm the director now. You may have done things differently in the past, but what relevance does that have?"

At this refutation, the third-year students were silenced.

"And you don't have to think of this as an obstacle. If the third-year students are more skilled than the first-years, there won't be a problem, will there? Am I wrong?"

This struck Kumiko as playing dirty. When Taki put it that way, the third-year students had no choice but to shut up and take it, since arguing further would be a tacit admission that the first-year students were better than they were.

Kaori hesitantly raised her hand. "Um, how will the auditions work?"

"I'll be distributing sheet music today, and I'd like you to practice it. You'll be tested on both the compulsory and free pieces," Taki said. "I'll be deciding solo assignments based on the audition as well, so bear that in mind."

Now the classroom was truly in an uproar. Solo sections were places in the score where a single player would play the melody or some other part of the song alone, or even create a new melody entirely. There were many ways to decide who got to play those parts, but Kitauji had always assigned solos by seniority. Taki's words upended that. If solos weren't going to be decided by class year, it was obvious that at least some of them would go to first-years instead of third-years.

Kaori glanced in Reina's direction with eyes full of uncertainty. Whether or not she noticed that, Reina's gaze was fixed solely on Taki.

"With the Class A band capped at fifty-five members, I will have anyone who I determine isn't playing at the Class A level moved to the Class B ensemble. This could mean the Class A band would end up being fewer than fifty-five, so I'll ask you all to practice hard and do the very best you can. Speaking of which, here is your schedule up until the audition," said Taki as he passed out a sheet crammed with practice assignments.

Kumiko involuntarily winced at the packed schedule. It made her dizzy just looking at it.

"This is amazing..." murmured—who else?—Asuka. Most Saturdays and Sundays had band practice scheduled, and days without any practice were few and far between. It was definitely going to be an imposition on the third-year students, who also had to be studying for college entrance exams.

Realizing this, Kumiko looked up with a quick intake of breath—she had just remembered Aoi. What would Aoi do? And just as the thought occurred to Kumiko, Aoi herself raised her hand.

"Er, may I say something?" said Aoi.

"What is it?" Taki cocked his head.

Aoi glanced down at the sheet of paper in her hand, then took a deep breath. With her slim fingers, she crumpled the gray-tinged paper. "I'm quitting band."

There was a murmured "Wha?" of surprise from Ogasawara, whose eyes went wide.

"Do you have a reason?" asked Taki, his voice as calm as ever.

Aoi's lips stiffened at the director's serious expression. "I need to put more effort into my entrance exam preparation. If I continue with band, I won't be able to get into my first-choice college. I've been thinking about it for a while, but it would be bad for the band if I were to quit after the audition, so I've decided to do it now."

"Aoi, please don't quit!" came the murmurs of her sad-faced juniors in the saxophone section. The reaction made it clear just how well-liked she was.

"...I see," said Taki, looking down. He brought a large hand to his cheek and let slip a too-deep, conflicted sigh. Then he straightened, as though bringing his emotions under control. "Understood. We'll do the necessary paperwork at a later date, so please come by the teachers' office this Monday, if you can."

"Yes, sir. I'm sorry to be causing trouble."

"It's quite all right. This is your decision, so please see it through. And good luck on your entrance exams."

"Thank you very much," replied Aoi, bowing deeply.

After a lengthy silence, Aoi came back up. Her expression was pleasant, but it had a lonely sadness to it. She unhooked her bag from the desk where it hung and began to walk toward the classroom's exit. Some of the first-year saxes were crying.

Aoi reached out to slide the door open, then looked back over her shoulder. Her gaze was directed at Asuka, who evenly returned it without a trace of emotion. She displayed not the slightest hint of sympathy for a departing band member. The tension in Aoi's lips suddenly faded, and when she finally left the room, there was no regret on her face at all.

A sudden urge welled up within Kumiko—she had to catch Aoi. It was an impatient emotion, with a sense of obligation mixed into it as well. There was a clatter as legs caught the edge of a chair, and in some part of her mind, Kumiko realized that she herself was the source of the sounds, for she had bolted to her feet.

"Wait, Aoi!"

Kumiko's body seemed to move on its own. She left the music classroom as though she'd been chased out. Hazuki's voice followed behind her, trying to stop her, but Kumiko pretended she didn't hear it.

"Aoi! Wait, please!" Someone else reached Aoi before Kumiko: Ogasawara. Maybe she'd left the music classroom first. She stood in front of Aoi, short of breath and unconcerned with her skirt's flipped-up hem. "Wait!"

"…" Aoi's brows furrowed in consternation. Kumiko hid herself to avoid being noticed. It seemed like a bad moment to intrude upon.

"Are you really quitting band?"

"Yeah."

"Why?"

"I said, didn't I? I've gotta study for exams," said Aoi, her gaze askance.

Ogasawara folded her arms and glared at Aoi. "If the practice is too tough, just play in Class B."

"I'd feel bad for the kids who're really working hard."

"So just play in the regular recital! That's when the third-years are retiring, anyway, so just hang in there until then!"

"I can't."

"Why not?"

"Because I..." Aoi's expression twisted. The two girls' shadows fell starkly on the white-painted hallway. It was bright outside, but the space they occupied felt somehow dim. The shouts of the baseball team floated in as they practiced outside on the athletics field. They seemed to come from a distant world, and it felt like this particular hallway was somehow separated from the rest of existence. The two girls were drowning inside that invisible membrane.

Ogasawara did not look away from Aoi. Aoi looked at the floor, as though trying to escape the gaze.

"I'm just not that in love with band." The words seemed to leak reluctantly from her throat. She bit her lip as though trying to keep them back. Her cheeks glowed red. "I've been wanting to quit for a while, honestly. I hate it." She spat the words out.

Ogasawara gasped. She recoiled, retreating one step back, then another.

Aoi grabbed her wrist. "Haruka— You remember what happened last year, too, don't you?"

"...I—"

"So you can't give me this 'Oh, ha-ha, we'll aim for Nationals' stuff. Why is everyone suddenly okay with this? I don't get it. After they attacked those girls last year."

"That was..."

"I can't do it. I can't take this. They've got no right to tell me, 'Well, I'm gonna work hard!' And they shouldn't be telling you that, either, Haruka."

Ogasawara said nothing in response. Her long ponytail swayed to and fro.

Aoi huffed, then roughly dropped Ogasawara's wrist. Ogasawara did not react, her eyes fixed dimly at the floor.

"It's good timing, anyway. No matter what I think, it's true that I have to study for entrance exams. I would've had to quit band regardless. Enough, okay?" said Aoi brusquely, and began to walk away. She showed no hesitation or regret, which gave the president no right to try to stop her.

Ogasawara didn't move. She was not going to follow Aoi.

"Aoi!" Kumiko called out in spite of herself. Aoi turned in surprise to see the figure that had suddenly emerged from hiding.

"Kumiko...? What're you doing here?"

"You said you were quitting, so I..." Kumiko wondered if they suspected her of eavesdropping. She awkwardly trailed off in midsentence.

Aoi sighed, a faint smile flickering across her face. "You were worried about me? Thanks." Her voice was kind, completely unlike the sharp tirade she'd spat just moments earlier. Ogasawara looked slowly up, her eyes turning toward Kumiko.

"Oumae, the club's in the middle of a meeting. What are you doing here?"

Aoi's eyes narrowed ever so slightly in amusement. "I could ask you the same thing, Haruka. What's the band president doing here? You should get back."

"Maybe, but..."

"You too, Kumiko—don't make trouble for other people. You should get back to the music room."

The words were kindly spoken, but there was an unmistakable rejection within them. Aoi was obscuring her true feelings behind many layers. *Is that what you really think, Aoi?* Kumiko would've been able to easily ask the simple question any other time, but now it stuck in her throat.

"Well...bye," said Aoi, finally turning and walking away from the two other girls. The slim line of her body was clear past the deep blue fabric of her uniform. The ruddy flush of her thighs flashed behind the sway of her skirt. There was no hesitation in her steps. All Kumiko could do was watch her go.

Once Aoi was gone, silence fell in the hallway. Kumiko was alone with the president, who hadn't moved a muscle in some time. With no idea what to do, Kumiko glanced hesitantly in the other girl's direction.

Ogasawara didn't look up. "...I knew it," she finally murmured softly.

Kumiko's ears caught the quiet voice.

"I knew I never should've been president," said Ogasawara, sinking to the floor on the spot. The sudden movement put her hair into a tangle, but then she was still again. Through the gaps in where her black hair fell over her shoulders, Kumiko could see the pale line of her neck. There was an angry red swelling there, too, and Kumiko wondered if a bug had bitten her or something.

"...President?" Kumiko said, hesitation in her voice. Ogasawara did not look up. Kumiko saw her hands grasping the hem of her skirt and trembling. "Are...are you all right?"

Kumiko laid a timid hand on the band president's shoulder. Still, she did not look up.

"If Asuka had been the president, Aoi wouldn't have quit."

"That is not true!" Kumiko said, the words' unavoidable stiltedness making them useless as consolation.

Ogasawara shrank further into herself at hearing the hollow formality. "Whatever, I know it's true. I'm nothing like Asuka. I'm not good at anything. I knew from the very beginning that I couldn't cut it at an important job like president. Everyone was thinking it—'Why couldn't Asuka have been president, instead of this screw-up?'"

"N-no one was thinking that!"

"Don't bother denying it. Even I notice that much." Ogasawara's voice was becoming more and more depressed.

"You have all kinds of good points that Asuka doesn't! All of us juniors think so."

"Name one, then!" shot back Ogasawara, just when Kumiko was starting to think she'd made some kind of an impression on the president.

Kumiko flinched as she fumbled for words. "Um, like how you're always so kind and considerate..."

"Besides that."

"Besides that...I mean, you always make sure to say hello to the juniors, and you're really nice..."

"What else?"

"Um…Oh! Like how it's so nice of you to sometimes bring snacks and stuff!"

"Great, so I'm nice and that's it!" Ogasawara stood, her eyes flashing.

Kumiko shrank away at the rebuke's intensity. Ogasawara's already tight eyes were puffy and red, making them seem even tighter. "'Nice' is what you call someone who doesn't have anything worthwhile about them! Don't think I don't know that!"

Kumiko was stunned into silence by the finger that Ogasawara furiously pointed at her. So this was who she really was. Suddenly Riko's words faded into being in her mind: *Ogasawara doesn't really have the right mind-set.*

Ogasawara continued to glare at Kumiko for a few seconds, then finally dropped her gaze to the floor. Her lowered eyelashes trembled, the shadow cast by her bangs falling gloomily across her red-tinged cheeks. Her always-composed face was contorted with emotion. "I'm just… I'm just…!"

A pair of arms appeared from behind Ogasawara. Ten fingers grabbed onto her shoulders. "God, are you moaning about this *again*?"

Ogasawara flinched bodily at the shock of being grabbed. Kumiko's eyes went wide at the sudden appearance of another person. "A-Asuka?!"

"Hm? Yes?" Asuka peered out from behind Ogasawara's shoulder as though nothing unusual was happening at all.

Ogasawara herself looked back and gave a strangled cry of surprise at finding Asuka's visage at point-blank range. "Wh-when did you…?"

"Hmm. I guess just a second ago. You guys were taking so long getting back that I came to get you," said Asuka. The corners of her lip curled up into a smile. "So, what're you two talking about here? I figured you'd just gone to try to stop Aoi, but…"

"Oh, Aoi—that is, er, she already left," said Kumiko.

"So, what, Haruka's just been arguing with you this whole time?"

"I'm not arguing!" disputed a red-faced Ogasawara.

Asuka gave a low, amused chuckle and pressed a finger up to the president's lips. "Now, now, Haruka. You've gotta get your emotions under control. You're the club president, after all."

"Oh, shut up!" snapped Ogasawara, turning away.

"I do kind of like it when you don't, though," murmured a grinning Asuka into her ear.

Ogasawara's facial expression boiled over instantly. "D-don't be stupid!"

"Aw, you love it."

"I do not!"

Despite Haruka's vehement denial, it was plain as day that she was now just trying to cover up her embarrassment. Evidently the concert band president was feeling better. Kumiko sighed in relief.

In what seemed like a very well-practiced gesture, Asuka gave Haruka a nudge with her hand. "Come on now, let's go back."

"I know, already!"

Ogasawara moved as she'd been encouraged to. Asuka really was a skilled cajoler, Kumiko mused vaguely as she followed behind the two girls.

Asuka said something. Ogasawara argued with it. Asuka laughed. This was their usual amicable dynamic; the earlier surprised despondency was nowhere to be seen, and Ogasawara's affect had returned to normal. Beside her, Asuka narrowed her eyes happily.

Then those clear eyes glanced back for just an instant. They were shockingly cold. Kumiko gulped and felt her heart lurch in her chest. It was a jarringly incongruous moment that interrupted the otherwise pure scene of two girls happy in their friendship.

"What's wrong, Kumiko?" Asuka looked back properly, noticing that Kumiko had stopped in her tracks.

Kumiko forced a smile to her face and shook her head. "Oh, um, n-nothing!"

"Oh? Well, that's good," said Asuka, turning to look ahead again. Kumiko tried to calm her pounding heart as she followed behind.

"Saitou's really quitting?" asked Shuuichi as he leaned back in the train bench.

The band had been dismissed shortly after Kumiko, Asuka, and Ogasawara had returned to the room. Kumiko had been standing on the train platform, alone with her uneasy thoughts, and it was Shuuichi who'd called out to her and suggested they go home together. Now that she thought of it, she was pretty sure that this was the first time she'd ridden the train with him. Kumiko shrugged as she traced her finger over the seat's green upholstery.

"I think so. Aoi's pretty serious."

"So not even the combo of Tanaka and President Ogasawara could convince her?"

The train clattered over its tracks. The scenery outside moved from right to left through its frame. Shuuichi put his bag on his lap and yawned.

Kumiko looked quietly down. "Asuka...wasn't trying to convince her in the first place."

"But she left after you and the president went to get Saitou. I was sure Tanaka'd gone to stop her, too."

"No, Asuka, she..."

That was as far as Kumiko got before she cut herself off with a quick intake of breath. What had Asuka wanted to say back there? Kumiko pressed her hands against her forehead. All that came to mind were Asuka's eyes in that moment. Those two bright eyes were superficially kind, but in their depths was something else—something unreadable but distinctly cold. Even now, Kumiko found them somehow terrifying.

"Asuka, she...what?" asked Shuuichi, head tilted curiously.

"Nothing," said Kumiko, shaking her head.

The two fell into silence. The train rattled, swaying as it rolled through a curve in the tracks.

"Man, I..." started Shuuichi. Kumiko looked up and over at him. She glimpsed the nape of his neck where it emerged from his uniform jacket's collar. Its line was—faintly, but distinctly—more robustly masculine than it had been in middle school. "I'm really... not a fan of hers."

"'Her'? Who do you mean?"

"Tanaka," said Shuuichi, scowling.

Kumiko was shocked into momentary silence. "D-don't ever say that in the band! They'll tear you apart if you say anything bad about Asuka!"

"You think I don't know how popular she is?"

"Okay, so why are you telling me this all of a sudden? And wait, didn't you really respect her at first?"

"Yeah, but...like...she's too perfect."

"Huh?" Kumiko blurted at the unexpected statement.

"It's like, you need faults, or...maybe you don't understand."

"I do not," said Kumiko immediately.

Shuuichi scratched his head, seemingly at a loss. "Well, try a little harder, then."

"I have no idea what you're talking about, though."

Shuuichi furrowed his brow. "I mean, I just hate that whole 'I'm totally perfect!' thing she does. Don't you think people in the band buy into that a little too much?"

"Oh, so you're just jealous."

"Oh, excuse me for being jealous, then!" snapped Shuuichi, turning away.

Kumiko smirked and smacked his shoulder. "I do kind of get it, though."

"Huh?" Shuuichi's eyes widened at the unexpected response. "What?"

"No, I just figured you were a true believer in Tanaka."

"I mean, I definitely respect her. She's really impressive as a senior band member. But..." Kumiko paused. She chose her words carefully, not wanting to say anything accidentally inflammatory. "I don't think she's exactly the person everybody thinks she is. She's not just nice and funny. It's more like she's—thinking on a different level."

"Like she's got her eyes on something else?"

"Yeah, something like that."

That was surely why Kumiko had found her eyes so frightening. The world she saw and the world Asuka saw were profoundly different places.

"Maybe that's it," murmured Shuuichi. The sunlight coming through the window limned his profile. A trace of facial hair had been left just beneath his nose. He kept nervously running his bony fingers to and fro over the top of his schoolbag. It was somehow suffocating to watch, and Kumiko reflexively looked away.

Clack, clack. Clack, clack, came the sound of the train on the rails.

"Hey, Kumiko. The trombone, Tsukamoto—are you going out with him?"

The jaunty question sauntered into Kumiko's ear, whereupon the bite of rolled egg omelet she'd been about to eat tumbled helplessly from her chopsticks' grasp. It fell to her desk's surface, yellow and white and tragic.

"...What?" Kumiko finally managed to answer, her brain spinning at a feverish pitch. Who the hell was "Tsukamoto"? And then she realized—the surname referred to Shuuichi.

"Like I said, are you going out with Tsukamoto?" Both Hazuki's and Midori's eyes sparkled brightly as they waited for Kumiko's answer.

The classroom was noisy with students' conversations. It had become daily routine now for the trio of Kumiko, Hazuki, and Midori to push their desks together next to the window and eat lunch together. Midori had a fancy-looking sandwich she'd bought at the bakery, Hazuki a convenience store rice ball, and Kumiko was eating a lunch her mother had packed for her. So far their conversation had been pleasant as usual, but that was before the aforementioned bomb was lobbed into its midst.

"Uh, no, we're not."

"Aw, that's no fun," pouted Midori, while beside her Hazuki breathed out a sigh of relief.

"Why do you ask?" said Kumiko.

"Oh, just that me and Hazuki were on the train, and we saw you guys together."

"That day we had band, you mean?"

"Yeah!" Midori nodded innocently. She looked over to Hazuki with a carefree smile. "Good news, right?"

"Wh-what's good about it?!" objected Hazuki, her face going red.

Kumiko ignored this and addressed Midori. "Good news?"

Midori giggled. "I figured something out!" she said, straightening proudly. Next to her, Hazuki flailed and grabbed her arm.

"Midori, wait—"

"Hazuki's got a thing for Tsukamoto!"

Kumiko's breath caught. Her mind went blank, and she couldn't think of what to say in response.

"Geez, why'd you have to say it?!"

"Aw, c'mon!" said Midori. The pair was completely oblivious to Kumiko's state as they bantered. "But honestly, I'm just relieved you and Kumiko didn't wind up in a love triangle."

"Anyway, it's not like I'm super into Tsukamoto! I'm just...sorta interested, that's all."

"Which means you *are* into him! Hah, I've got it all figured out." Midori was delighted. She was notably susceptible to discussing romantic relationships, perhaps because she'd gone to all-girl schools for both elementary and middle school. "But anyway, Kumiko, why were you going home together? Are you and Tsukamoto friends or something?"

"Ah, yeah. My mom and Shuuichi's mom have known each other for a long time, and our families have spent a lot of time together ever since I moved here in third grade, so you could call us childhood friends."

"Oh! Lucky you, having a childhood friend. I want one."

"Why don't you make one?"

"You can't just 'make' a childhood friend!" pouted Midori. Poking her puffed-out cheeks only made her sulkier. Next to Midori, Hazuki was gazing absentmindedly at Kumiko.

"Hazuki?" The words seemed to bring her back to herself, and she stiffened. "What's up?"

"Oh, uh, n-nothing, really." Hazuki shook her head with an expression that strongly suggested it was not "nothing." Midori seemed to notice this, too, and an evil grin spread across her face.

"Hazuki's got a problem, see—how to invite Tsukamoto to the Agata Festival."

"Midori, god! Why do you have to keep shooting your mouth off!"

Midori giggled. "Aw, don't be like that."

The Agata Festival Midori referred to was the festival of the Agata Shrine, which was held on June fifth every year, with festivities running until dawn on the sixth. Late in the night, the streetlights would be extinguished, and a great float carrying a Brahma would pass through in the dark, which gave the event its nickname, "the mysterious festival of the dark night."

"So who are *you* going with, then?!" demanded the blushing Hazuki.

Midori smiled. "I'm going with my mom. We go together every year!"

"You're going with your mom?"

"Sure am. I get along great with my mom," said Midori merrily.

Kumiko was utterly defeated. Going to a festival with her parents—at her age!—was unimaginable.

Hazuki seemed to feel much the same way, and her earlier vehemence evaporated entirely as she waved her hand side to side dismissively as if to say, *Aw, forget it.*

"What about you, Kumiko?" asked Midori.

"Hmm. It's kind of a pain. I might not go at all."

Midori's eyes went wide with surprise at this answer. She smacked her hand on her desk repeatedly to express her dissatisfaction. "It's gonna be a whole festival! What a waste not to go!"

"Y-you think so?"

"Yes, a waste. You should definitely, definitely go."

Midori subsequently and enthusiastically advised that Kumiko ought to attend with her and her mother—a proposal that Kumiko politely declined.

The piece Taki had selected for the band's free performance, "East Coast Pictures," had been composed for wind ensemble by Nigel Hess. The work had been written based on Hess's impressions during a visit to the East Coast of the United States and was a three-movement composition on the subject of New York and its surroundings. The first movement was on Shelter Island, the second, the Catskill Mountains, and the third, New York City itself.

Performing all three movements would easily exceed the competition's time limit, so Taki had decided to play the first movement in its entirety but only selections from the second and third movements. The highlight of the second movement was definitely the cornet solo.

The cornet was an instrument sometimes played by trumpet performers in place of their usual instrument. It was constructed very differently from the trumpet, with a conical bore instead of a cylindrical bore, but because its playing technique and range were very similar to the trumpet's, in the modern era it was often treated as a member of the trumpet family. Kumiko assumed that someone from the trumpet section would be playing the cornet solo. The movement in question had been written to convey the tranquil but nonetheless majestic grandeur of the Catskill mountain range.

The third movement was meant to capture the energy and clamor of New York City's Manhattan, and its centerpiece had to be the sirenlike wails that evoked the city's ambulances and fire engines, which rang out in the piece's final crescendo. It was like a musical stage production in vignette form, full of narrative and splendor.

"It's just so cool…!" murmured Asuka breathily as she gazed at the sheet music during sectional practice.

Behind her, Takuya stared grimly at a different piece of sheet music as he carefully wrote numbers of some kind on it. When Kumiko looked more closely, she saw that the music was for "Copacabana."

"Um, what are you doing?" Kumiko asked Takuya.

He slowly looked up. "…I'm writing the fingerings down for Katou."

"Hazuki's going to play that?"

"Looks like it. Guess for Class B they're gonna do 'Copacabana' with Ms. Michie directing. We've got a lot of people in the percussion section now, so most of 'em are going to end up in Class B. It's a good tune, considering the instrument lineup they'll have."

Natsuki poked her face over Kumiko's shoulder, leering at the "Copacabana" sheet music at which Takuya was so intently staring. Both the eupho and the tuba were bass instruments, so music for each was written in the bass clef. Every day, Hazuki would be playing music that was written with notes that she'd hardly ever encountered before. Once she got used to it, she'd be able to read them as quickly as she looked at them, but while she was still a novice, it would remain difficult. So Takuya was writing the scale positions and fingerings in for her.

"Kumikoooo, how can you even play from this sheet music?" cried a defeated Hazuki, who had just finished getting some pointers from Riko. Behind her, Midori was absorbed in her fundamental drills.

"Well, the eupho and the tuba are different. And strictly speaking I've never played *that* music."

"Same difference, though! And it's a bass, too."

"Yeah, well, the contrabass is also a bass! So go bother Midori!"

Riko smiled pleasantly at the busily drilling Midori. "She's really amazing, isn't she?"

"Heh, thanks!" said Midori, pleased, before turning her attention back to her practice. Her tiny fingertips plucked a string, and the foot-tingling bass note rippled out into the room.

Having finished her own fundamentals practice, Kumiko turned her attention to "Crescent Moon Dance," the sheet music she'd been given. The piece's most notable qualities were the opening trumpet melody and the latter half's bass melody. Euphonium, tuba, contrabass—normally these were all instruments that stayed in the background, but here they were suddenly in the spotlight. The bass section was active throughout the entire composition, and the euphonium part was especially brutal. There were no long rests, and, not counting the opening trumpet fanfare, they played throughout nearly the entire piece. Bands were allowed to choose their compulsory performance from among five options, but this one was overwhelmingly the most difficult. And it was long.

The band's level did not, broadly speaking, match the song's.

...Can we really pull it off?

Kumiko unconsciously frowned. Taki's words from the other day ran through her mind.

"We decided on this compulsory piece because it will be difficult for you. I look forward to your most sincere efforts precisely because of that difficulty. You might be tempted to underperform with an easier piece. But if you can perform both this compulsory and this free piece perfectly, then Nationals will not be a mere dream."

The National Concert Band Competition.

Kumiko whispered the words to herself, sighing. Sitting nearby was Asuka, playing through a difficult passage as though it was no big deal. This ought to have been Asuka's first time seeing this sheet music, but there was no hesitation in her playing. Kumiko supposed it came down to a difference in fundamental talent. Asuka could look at the sheet music and immediately reproduce the notes' sound—that was how thoroughly she understood the eupho.

After playing through a simple-looking section, Kumiko examined the beamed note groups of a difficult melody elsewhere. She knew it was flatly impossible to play them at the specified tempo right away. Kumiko got her metronome out and set the tempo significantly lower. She listened carefully to the regular *tick, tick* sound, then played through the run of notes at about a third their proper speed. She had to understand first her fingers' movements, then her mouth's. As she became more comfortable with those, she could gradually increase the speed to approach the original tempo.

Repeat, and repeat again. She played the phrase over and over. And as she did so, the difficult music began to sink into her fingers. Kumiko found she quite liked the feeling of something impossible becoming possible.

"You're pretty good."

Kumiko stopped playing and looked back to see who'd addressed her. It was Natsuki, who regarded her with an even gaze.

Kumiko was unused to straightforward praise. "Um, thank you."

She felt heat rise to her face and gave a light bow to hide it. She saw Natsuki's face reflected askew in her instrument's flaking golden finish.

"So when'd you start playing eupho?"

"In fourth grade. I joined the brass band."

"So this is what, your seventh year? Yeah, that'd make a difference," said Natsuki with a self-conscious smile. What did she mean by "difference"? Kumiko's head was filled with question marks, but Natsuki just chuckled amusedly. "Nah, don't worry about it."

It was only much later that Kumiko would come to understand what Natsuki meant by that.

Midori had cram school. Hazuki had gone home with another friend. So Kumiko made her way toward the school's front gate alone. The school bustled at the sounding of the bell that signaled the end of the day's extracurricular activities. Mouthpieces were washed and instruments returned to their cases. And once the wave of departing students had passed, silence fell over the campus. Summer's approach meant that there was time before the sun set, but the dimming school grounds were nonetheless far from cheerful.

As Kumiko retrieved her loafers from their shoe locker, a voice called out to her. "Whoa, you're just now heading home, too?"

She looked back to see Shuuichi wave to her. Evidently he was leaving—he held his trombone case by its handle.

"Oh, I was just thinking of doing some practice at home," said Shuuichi, seemingly bashful at Kumiko's observation of his instrument.

"How's the compulsory coming?"

"Eh, so-so. My problem now is the tone when I come in after the trumpets. What about the euphs?"

"I mean, obviously the melody in the second half is terrifying."

"Yeah, that's nuts," said Shuuichi with a laugh, shoving his school slippers roughly into his own shoe locker. His own shoes were much larger than Kumiko's. There wasn't anything surprising about that, but she was strangely caught off guard by the detail. Suddenly feeling a tightness in her chest, she looked away.

"Think you'll make it through the audition?" she asked.

"I wonder. There are a lot of trombones, so I might be headed to Class B."

"How many are there in the trombone section, again?"

"Seven. There's one beginner, so six of us are going to be auditioning."

"That's rough."

The bass section was small to begin with, so it was possible they'd all pass. The compulsory piece needed the bass, so even if it made the band larger, Kumiko couldn't imagine the bass section shrinking.

They passed through the school's front gate and continued on along the gently sloping road to the station. Tea fields were visible at regular intervals as they walked along the asphalt road. Views of verdant fields were not too remarkable to Uji residents, however.

"I'm kinda glad I came to this school," said Shuuichi.

"Where'd *that* come from?"

"No, I mean, I just realized it during sectionals." He smiled. "At first I thought the band was just crap, but lately everybody's actually started to take practice seriously."

"The Mr. Taki Effect at work, you think?"

"That's part of it, but it's not just that." A warm breeze blew past the pair, and Shuuichi smiled awkwardly. He looked down to the case that hung from his right hand. "We got all those compliments at the SunFest. 'Wow, Kitauji's gotten good,' and all that. That felt really good. It made me think that maybe we really are getting better." He let slip a shy little chuckle.

Kumiko nodded her agreement. "It's starting to sink in that we can actually do this."

"Yeah, and that's the fun part. Like, 'Whoa, if we actually put the work in...'"

The sun was setting, the last vestiges of its light leaving reluctant scratches across the sky as it sank. Faded red blurred into deep blue. The sense of evening's arrival began to suffuse the air. Streetlights flickered on as though in defiance of the dark, and Shuuichi's form cast a palely jutting shadow.

"I wonder if we'll make it to Nationals," he said. Kumiko watched his profile. He seemed to notice, and looked away self-consciously. "What?"

"No, um... Yeah. I'd like to go to Nationals, too."

"Instead of pulling a repeat of what happened in middle school."

—*I hate it. I hate it so much I could die.*

That moment, Reina had cried. Kumiko hadn't, because she'd honestly thought the gold prize was good enough. Not Reina, though. Reina had sincerely thought they could go to Nationals. And she'd badly wanted to.

"I want to get better," said Kumiko. She'd meant to say it quietly, but there in the evening street her words echoed with surprising volume.

Shuuichi looked briefly taken aback, but then grinned with pleasure, his white teeth flashing. "Let's practice together sometime soon. On the river path or somewhere. So we can both make it to Class A."

"Ugh, bringing my eupho home is a huge pain."

"Way to ruin the moment! Try to read the mood a little, huh?"

"I'm serious, though," said Kumiko, smacking Shuuichi's back in retort with a dry *slap* sound. "But I guess we can hang out for practice, at least," she continued.

The words made her feel suddenly self-conscious, and she quickened her stride as though to escape. The station was close, and as Kumiko hurried ahead of him, Shuuichi broke into a hasty trot to catch up.

As the dates of the audition approached, the mood in the band grew tenser and tenser. It was quieter, too; everyone was too busy staring down at their sheet music for the usual idle chatter. If you went to the staff room, you could count on seeing a gaggle of students with questions for Taki gathered around his desk. It was all Taki could do to smile awkwardly at the rest of the faculty's dryly amused remarks about how motivated the concert band seemed to be this year.

Every ensemble practice increased the notes scribbled on the sheet music. Kumiko eyed the margins, which were increasingly overwhelmed with pencil marks, then regarded the instrument in her arms. The veteran euphonium's plating was flaking off in places. She set it down on the floor, then took out a handkerchief and stood.

"You're going to be fine!" a familiar voice exclaimed just as Kumiko entered the girls' bathroom. It was Yuuko and Kaori, both trumpets, standing in front of the sinks outside as they discussed something. They took no notice of Kumiko.

"I dunno, I really think Reina's just better than me."

"That's not true! You're definitely better than she is, Kaori!" Even from inside a stall, Kumiko could hear the conversation clearly.

"I wonder if Reina's going to get the solo, though."

"No way, it'd be ridiculous for a third-year not to play the solo!"

"You say that, but…"

"You should *definitely* get the solo, Kaori." There was a dull *thud*—evidently Yuuko had stomped her foot.

"Well, I'll do the best I can, anyway," said Kaori, her voice distinctly gloomy.

"Yes! And I'll be there to cheer you on!" Kumiko heard Yuuko reply as the voices grew distant. When she opened the stall door, no one was there.

With the day's band activities over, Kumiko washed her mouth-piece at the large outdoor sink. The silver-colored metal piece glittered in the stream of water. A pleasant memory from elementary school came to her—filling her own cup with the hot green tea that issued straight out of a special faucet. She'd been surprised to learn that the installation was unique to Uji, which was famous for its tea.

"Hey," came a voice from behind Kumiko. She turned to see Shuuichi there, holding his own mouthpiece. Trombone sectionals must have just ended.

"Rinsing your mouthpiece?"

"Yeah," he said, without further elaboration. Kumiko wondered what was wrong. She turned her head to look at him. Standing next to her at the sink, he took a deep breath.

"Hey—are you free on the fifth?" he asked. He looked truly awful—the words "deathly pallor" came to mind.

"Huh? That's a weekday, right? We'll have band."

"No, I mean after that!"

"After band?" Kumiko suddenly realized what he was getting at. "Oh, is this about the Agata Festival?"

Shuuichi's face reddened visibly. Kumiko wondered what *that* was about. Her own face warmed as though infected with whatever it was. Normally she wouldn't have even noticed the distance between them, but for some reason it felt extremely close. She restrained the sudden urge to flee and forced herself to act normally.

Still looking down, Shuuichi replied quietly, "...I was wondering if you'd want to go with me."

"Ah, um..."

Kumiko was about to answer *Sure*, but then Hazuki emerged from the instrument storage room and entered her field of vision. The full-body flush she felt was instantly replaced with a cold sweat.

Hazuki's got a thing for Tsukamoto! Midori's words from earlier flashed through Kumiko's mind. *Crap, this is bad!* she thought, and her body reacted on its own. She reflexively grabbed the arm of the student who just happened to be passing by. "Sorry! I can't, I'm going with her!"

"...What?" came an irritated-sounding voice. Kumiko looked up with a quick intake of breath and saw that the arm she'd grabbed belonged to none other than Reina. Kumiko's already-wide eyes opened still further.

Reina's entire body radiated an aura of displeasure, as if to say *What the hell are you talking about?*

"Oh. You're going with Kousaka, then..."

"Y-yeah."

It was an unthinkable combination, Kumiko and Reina, but Shuuichi seemed not even slightly dubious at the assertion. He was probably too nervous for his brain to be functioning properly. "Ah, okay. Too bad," he said with an empty little chuckle.

An irritated Reina looked at Shuuichi and Kumiko in turn but said nothing. Maybe she'd understood the situation.

"Hey, Tsukamoto!" said Hazuki, trotting up behind him. Kumiko noticed the faint color on her cheeks, and her heart groaned, a heavy feeling churning in her chest. She tightened her grip on Reina's arm to endure it. Reina frowned briefly at this but kept silent.

"Katou?" Shuuichi tilted his head, puzzled.

Hazuki grabbed Shuuichi's arm as she approached, seemingly to give her empty hands something to do. His left arm settled naturally into the grasp of her sun-browned hands. "I wanna talk. C'mere."

"Uh, I was just talking with Kumiko, though."

Shuuichi looked to her, and Kumiko forced a smile to her face, tightening her grip on Reina's arm. "Oh, I'm fine! Go on!"

Kumiko saw the obvious flicker of his eyes. Her breath caught. Shuuichi opened his mouth, but all that came out was air. His unvoiced feelings slipped out of his big hands. Kumiko knew exactly how to rescue them. But she didn't move. She *couldn't* move.

"Seriously?" said Shuuichi, an angry note in his voice.

"Yeah, seriously. Go on." Kumiko looked away. The sunset-tinged early-evening air seeped in through the cracked window. The hallway was tinged with the light from the melting sun. There in the red-lit space, the boy turned away as though to escape.

"...Fine, then," he said, showing Kumiko his back.

Hazuki's and Shuuichi's voices grew fainter as they left. Kumiko heard a "What'd you want to talk about?" followed by an "Oh, nothing, just something I can't say here." From opposite the stairs came the echoes of a boy's and girl's mingling laughter.

Kumiko stood there, rooted to the spot. The mouthpiece in her hand was by now thoroughly warmed by her body heat.

"...Will that do?" said Reina quietly.

The words brought Kumiko back to the present with a start, and she let go of the other girl. "Sorry for dragging you into that."

"It's fine," said Reina, a guarded expression still on her face. Her lustrous black hair fell to her chest, obscuring most of her uniform's ribbon. In her arms, her star-colored trumpet glittered innocently. "So. What time do you want to meet up?"

"For what?"

"For the festival. I'm also free, so it's a good opportunity."

"Wha...? You're really going?"

"What are you talking about? Obviously I'm going. You just invited me."

"Well, yeah, but…"

"Then it's settled!" said Reina with a smile. Kumiko had never once seen her expression look like that before. She found herself mesmerized by it. The smile in Reina's eyes brightened a touch. Kumiko watched her long eyelashes flutter. *Wow, she's gorgeous*, she thought to herself, as though she'd only just noticed it.

After so much disciplined practice, the day of the Agata Festival brought a buoyant energy to the band. Snatches of cheerful conversation flew here and there—"When do you want to meet up?" "Are you gonna watch them carry the shrine palanquin?" "We should find somewhere to watch the fireworks!"—and Kumiko, too, felt a greater than usual need for some fun to blow off her pent-up nervous energy.

"Who are you going with?" Kumiko asked Asuka, who'd up until a moment earlier been absorbed in tracing her finger along a passage of her sheet music.

"I'm going with Kaori. She's my date," said Asuka amusedly.

"Oh, how nice," said Riko next to her, smiling.

"What about you, Riko?" asked Kumiko.

"Me? Um, I'm—"

"—Going with Gotou, obviously," interrupted Natsuki.

Riko blushed red. "Why do you have to be like that?"

"It's true, isn't it? You went together last year, too."

Kumiko reflexively glanced over at Takuya. He was practicing the compulsory as usual but had just fluffed several notes in a row. Apparently his usual calm had been disturbed.

"Oooh, are Riko and Goto gonna get all lovey-dovey?" said Midori, her eyes shining. Riko flushed at the words "lovey-dovey," which Natsuki ignored as she nodded firmly.

"You bet they are. They're an item, after all."

"Oooooo!" squealed Midori at the simply stated fact. "Riko! How could you not tell us something so important?!"

Kumiko had always thought that Takuya was interested in Asuka, so she inwardly sympathized with Midori's vehemence.

"I, um, I mean, it didn't seem worth going to the trouble of announcing..."

"And Gotou! You should've said something, too!"

Asuka smiled with chagrin as she placated her enthusiastic junior. "Now, now, Midori, you can't get mad at them just for being shy."

"If you say so..." pouted Midori with a reluctant nod.

"What about you, Natsuki? Going with anyone?" asked Asuka.

Natsuki answered with a deliberate shrug. "I've got cram school today."

"Hey, I'm a third-year and I'm going, so why're you stuck studying when you're still a second-year?"

"My parents are on me about it. Nothing I can do," said a frustrated Natsuki before she looked to Kumiko. "So what're you doing?"

"Oh, I'm going with Reina. The trumpet."

"Wait, Kumiko, I thought you said you weren't going to the festival?" said Midori, her head cocked. Behind her, Asuka stroked her chin thoughtfully.

"Reina... You don't mean that Kousaka girl, do you?"

"I don't know why you call her 'that girl,' but yes, her last name's Kousaka."

"So Kumiko, you're friends with Kousaka..." murmured Riko thoughtfully. Something in her tone gave Kumiko the impression that Riko somehow pitied her.

"...So, what about *this* space case?" said Natsuki, indicating Hazuki with a sardonic look. Hazuki sat with her tuba in her lap, an empty husk staring off into space, her mind clearly elsewhere.

"Hazuki's been like that all day," said Midori, lowering her voice conspiratorially. "She's going to the festival with her crush today. Apparently she's gonna tell him how she feels!"

"Whoa, that's like actual sweet summer romance! Makes me a little sick just hearing about it," said Natsuki, not bothering to hide her look of disgust. Her voice was plenty loud, but Hazuki showed no reactions. Evidently she couldn't hear.

"Her crush" had to mean Shuuichi. Kumiko exhaled, turning her attention away from the conversation. She felt unwell. Her stomach grumbled. She gripped her euphonium in an effort to calm the unpleasant roiling in her guts. *I don't like this. I don't like it.* She didn't have a precise reason for thinking so, but the emotion was there all the same.

"So long as it doesn't get in the way of band activities, you should feel free to pursue any dalliance or romance you like," said Asuka, deepening her smile.

"Do *you* have a boyfriend?" asked Midori, full of curiosity.

"What are you talking about? My eupho is my only love!" Asuka responded unequivocally.

"Aw, don't dodge the question," complained Midori, pouting, but Asuka only chuckled at her junior's antics.

As Kumiko watched, she couldn't help but feel that Asuka wasn't necessarily joking about her only love.

Kumiko had arranged to meet Reina in front of Uji Shrine at seven PM. The Agata Festival wasn't as huge as something like the Gion Festival, but it was still a respectably big event in its own right, with over six hundred street-side stalls and 120,000 people attending.

Now that she was thinking of it, Kumiko realized that this would be the first time she'd done anything fun with Reina. Since they'd been part of the same club in middle school, they'd naturally been acquaintances but never so friendly as to hang out. When they saw each other at school, they'd chat a little, and that was about it. It seemed to Kumiko, as she reflected, that Reina always kept some distance between herself and the people around her. She wasn't solitary per se, but she seemed averse to spending time with anyone in particular. That had held true in high school as well, and Kumiko had never seen Reina with a friend.

"Sorry to keep you waiting."

Kumiko turned at the voice that addressed her. There was Reina, wearing a youthfully feminine white dress. If Kumiko had been a boy, it was the kind of dress that would be at the top of the list of things she'd like her girlfriend to wear.

"Oh, no, I haven't been waiting," said Kumiko, looking askance. She felt suddenly inadequate next to the beautiful girl and wished she'd worn something better. She glanced down at the plain T-shirt and shorts she had on and sighed.

"Sighing as soon as I get here?" Reina frowned. The scowl suited her. "Are you that worried about Tsukamoto?"

"N-no—I mean, that's not how it is, with Shuuichi."

"Not how it is, huh?" said Reina with a meaningful glance.

Kumiko hurried to change the subject. "Let's get going. Is there anything special you want to eat?"

"I'm not interested in walking around the stalls. I hate crowds."

"Huh?"

"Let's go up Mt. Daikichi!" said Reina, pointing in the direction of the shrine. Kumiko wondered what the girl was suddenly talking about.

Grabbing the openmouthed Kumiko's hand, Reina began to hurry up the steps. The lamplight around them illuminated her slender, pale fingers, their pink nails neatly trimmed. Reina ignored Kumiko's scowl and produced her phone from her purse.

"Wh-why are we going up a mountain? I thought we were going to the festival."

"Hm? I dunno, it just seemed fun."

Reina snickered. Once they had passed Uji Shrine, the stone path continued up to Ujigami Shrine. Along with Byoudou-in, Ujigami Shrine had been designated a World Heritage Site in 1994, but the shrine received far fewer tourists than the temple. The three inner shrines in its main hall were the oldest ones in the world and incredibly valuable. To Kumiko's eyes, accustomed as they were to the show-offy sensibilities of modern architecture, they seemed rather plain.

"I love this shrine," said Reina, peering through a gap in the door.

"More than Uji Shrine? It's so much bigger," said Kumiko. Reina huffed in response.

"You just don't appreciate the understated."

"U-understated...?"

"You could call it 'mature charm,' I suppose."

"Are you saying Ujigami Shrine is more mature?"

"You know what I mean, though, don't you? Like, you can just feel it in the air."

"I guess…"

Now that she mentioned it, Kumiko couldn't deny that she felt *something* charming about the place. She scanned the silent, melancholy grounds of the shrine. On the other side of the bridge, people were swarming to the festival, but here it was disturbingly quiet. Reina and Kumiko were the only ones in the thick, choking silence. An inexplicable restlessness ate away at her consciousness little by little. What in the world was she doing here? Everyone else was going to the festival.

As Kumiko stared off into space, Reina grabbed her hand and set off again at a jaunty pace. A sky-blue scrunchie held her normally loose hair in a single ponytail.

"I'm not a fan of how bright it is."

"How bright what is?"

"The festival. It's just a big mess of glaring lights. I don't like it."

"Really?"

"Yeah. I hate it. It's depressing."

The farther they traveled down the path, the deeper the darkness became. The streetlights became fewer and fewer, until it was so dim they couldn't see far at all. There were no lamps on Mt. Daikichi itself. Kumiko frowned, but Reina ignored her and pulled her phone out of her bag.

"I thought it might be dark," she said, and turned on her phone to use it as a flashlight. Its pure white beam illuminated the path ahead. "I downloaded an app," said Reina with a smile, which Kumiko vaguely returned.

Locals called the mountain Mt. Daikichi, but it was properly known as Mt. Buttoku and was 131 meters tall at its summit. The path to the lookout point at the top started in a neighborhood filled with landmarks from the "Agemaki" chapter of *The Tale of Genji*, and its width and even grade made it a natural walking path, popular for its beautiful scenery. In the mornings it was frequented by people walking their dogs, and during preschool Kumiko had often been taken here for various outings.

"Do you do this kind of thing often?" Kumiko asked Reina as they walked.

Reina cocked her head curiously. "This kind of thing?"

"I mean, like, suddenly deciding to climb a mountain and stuff."

"What do you think I am? Of course not."

"R-right, of course."

Reina's sandal straps dug into her feet. The path up Mt. Daikichi wasn't staggeringly steep, but it was bad enough that heeled sandals weren't exactly the best choice.

"But sometimes I want to do stupid stuff like this," said Reina, rubbing her head self-consciously, like a kid whose secret had been found out. "I put on my uniform, I go to school, I go to band. Then I go home and study. After a while…I kinda just want to throw it all away. Just buy one of those Seishun 18 train passes during a holiday and travel somewhere, for no reason at all."

"I…kinda get that."

Kumiko longed to travel, to find herself. She often identified with the backpackers she occasionally saw on TV travel programs. There were days when she wanted to leap into a world where nobody knew anything about her. It was always fantasy, though, and no such plans had ever been put into action.

"I guess this is just a substitute for real travel."

"Pretty scaled back, though," said Kumiko.

"It is what it is. We've got school tomorrow," said Reina. Something about the expression on her face as she explained the obvious was funny, and Kumiko giggled. Reina glanced at her, then looked away.

"Honestly, I've wanted to for a while."

"Wanted to what?"

"Do something with you."

"Really?"

"Really."

Reina was looking ahead. Her ear was normally hidden behind

her hair, but today it was bared and visible. The skin was faintly colored and delicate. Kumiko found herself considering such absurdities as how soft it might feel if she were to bite it.

"You've actually got a pretty bad personality, Kumiko."

"Wha…" This was a shock. Ask anyone who had anything to do with her, and they'd tell you Kumiko was a good kid. A nice girl.

A nice girl. She'd imprinted on the phrase in early childhood. When had she started trying to force herself closer to that ideal?

Reina directed an enchanted smile at the silent Kumiko. "I've wanted to peel that good-girl skin right off you."

"………Is that an insult?"

"Not at all. I'm saying that's what I like about you. Call it a love confession."

"It's definitely not a love confession."

"Maybe you just don't understand my love."

"Nope, I don't." All Kumiko did understand was the delight on Reina's face as she doled out her teasing. The Reina she saw at school and the Reina she was looking at now were the same person, but they seemed utterly different.

"I wonder if you even remember, Kumiko."

"Remember what?"

The conversation continued as the pair walked.

"In middle school, what we talked about after the band competition."

"Sure, I remember that. When you cried, right?"

"Why do you even remember some other person crying? You really are bad."

"No way, that's totally normal!" protested Kumiko.

Reina smiled. "I'm just kidding. But when I was crying about how much I hated it, you came over and asked if I really thought we could've made it to Nationals."

"Did I say that?"

"You did. That's when I first thought, 'Wow, she's nasty.'"

"I-I mean, I was probably just…honestly curious about what you thought. I didn't have an ulterior motive!"

Reina grinned at the frantically backpedaling Kumiko. "I know.

That's what I liked about you. If you could honestly just ask something like that, you were just serious."

"Serious?"

"Seriously twisted."

"Come on, that's *definitely* an insult."

"I already told you it's not. I'm saying that's what I like about you!"

"Liar."

"It's true!" said Reina, her voice high and amused.

The lookout point would be coming into view soon. The pair continued confidently along their path. Kumiko looked down and saw Reina's sandals, now much dirtier than they had been before. There were angry marks on her pale skin where the straps had dug in.

"Don't your feet hurt?"

"They do," said Reina with a serious expression. "But I don't mind pain."

"That's kind of a sexy thing to say."

"...Don't be stupid."

Kumiko winced at the rough brush-off. As their empty banter continued, they finally reached the lookout point. It was situated about halfway up the mountain and afforded a view of most of the city of Uji.

"...It's gorgeous," murmured Reina as she gripped the handrails.

An artificial galaxy of stars—house lights, apartment lights, streetlights, car headlights—was sprinkled across the dark-painted world below. The city overflowed with light; from above it was like a great map spreading out before them. Here was Byoudou-in; there was Uji River. Kumiko exhaled as her eyes traced the city's lines to find familiar places.

"Is this what you wanted to see?"

Reina shook her head slightly. "It's not that I wanted to see this, exactly."

"What do you mean?"

Reina gave a teasing smile at Kumiko's questioning glance. Her strawberry-red tongue flicked out from between her lips. "I didn't want to do what everybody else was doing."

She looked back down at crowds leaving the festival area. They were a mass, all facing the same direction. Eating the same unexceptional candied apples, walking back to the train station full of self-satisfaction. And not far away, a rowdy crowd of middle schoolers, hair bleached the same shade of blond, each showing off their nonconformity in exactly the same way.

...But no, of course not. There was no way to see any of those things from this distance. From such a height, individual people dissolved into the darkness. The only things visible were the impassively shining lights.

"Nobody else would do something so dumb as climbing a mountain on a festival day, right?"

"I guess not," murmured Kumiko quietly.

"I just thought you might understand."

"Understand what?"

"This weird feeling."

Reina looked away.

"I do understand," said Kumiko. She wondered if Hazuki and Shuuichi were somewhere in that sea of light.

A butterfly came flittering creepily up in front of Kumiko. As a child she'd never shied away from touching butterflies, and she wondered when it was exactly that she'd started to find them creepy. She suppressed the urge to swat it away and smiled. "I know how you feel, Reina," she said.

Reina reached out and traced her finger along Kumiko's cheek. "I want to be special," she said.

"Special?"

"Yes. I want to be valued by others. I don't want people to think I'm the same as everybody else." The girl's hand fell limply to her side. Her white dress billowed in the breeze. "That's why I play the trumpet."

"You can be special if you play the trumpet?"

"I can," answered Reina without equivocation. "That's why I'm in the band. To be special. Why do you stay in band?"

Kumiko still didn't have an answer for that question. Reina let slip a small breath, then sat down on a bench. She crossed her long legs and folded her hands in her lap.

Kumiko let go of the lookout's handrails and sat beside Reina. A sweet scent tickled her nose.

"Kumiko—what made you start with concert band?"

"What was it, I wonder…" Her memories of so long ago were vague, the moments seeming to dissolve as soon as she seized upon anything clear. The day she first held an instrument. The day she learned what a euphonium was. What was it that had prompted her to join the brass band?

"I think…it was my older sister."

"Your sister? Kumiko, you have an older sister?"

"Yeah. We're nothing alike, though."

Kumiko's older sister had joined the brass band. She'd worn a sparkling uniform and played the trombone. That's right—that's why Kumiko had been so taken by the trombone. It was the wonderful instrument her sister had played. The way its slide zoomed in and out was so cool. She'd wanted to play one, so she'd joined the brass band, too. To be like her older sister. But then she'd ended up being assigned the euphonium.

"I think I joined the concert band because I looked up to my sister so much."

"Wow. Does she still play?"

"No, she quit in sixth grade. She said she wanted to go to a private middle school, so she was busy with cram school and stuff."

Kumiko's sister hadn't joined a club in middle school—or high school. She just did laps from home to school to cram school, going to and from the same places, over and over again.

"Exams," sniffed Reina with a disgusted look.

"That's gonna be our problem, too," said Kumiko.

"Yeah," said Reina, falling silent.

Kumiko wondered what she was thinking about. She, too, closed her mouth. The stillness swirled behind her eardrums, the man-made galaxy spreading out before her. Kumiko took in the sight, then softly closed her eyes. It was nice being with Reina. It felt like the first time she had experienced silence as anything besides stifling. She leaned her slender body back in the bench and stretched her legs out. Their arms linked, skin covering skin. Reina's touch was cool and pleasant, just slightly damp with sweat.

Red completion stamps accumulated on her practice schedule as the audition days approached. Kumiko boarded the last car in the train and made for a corner seat. The music player she produced from her bag had both the compulsory and free pieces on it.

Her fingers tapped against her bag, the fingerings for the valves' pistons having become muscle memory. When she looked up, she spotted Shuuichi a short distance away, listening to his own music. He brought his face up and glanced at her. Their eyes met for a moment, but he quickly averted his gaze. It had been like this ever since that day.

Shuuichi was avoiding Kumiko.

"What's *with* that girl?"

It was sectional practice. Natsuki's tone was distinctly annoyed when she asked the question and pointed at a dazed Hazuki. Hazuki, meanwhile, stared out the window, her cheek resting in her palm. Occasionally she would heave a great sigh, which seemed to have irritated Natsuki enough to move to a seat next to Kumiko's. Kumiko closed her folder of sheet music for the free piece and turned to face Natsuki.

"Do you have any idea?"

"No, I don't. I think Midori might, though."

Natsuki looked over to Midori at Kumiko's suggestion. Midori was absorbed in a staring contest with her sheet music, but when she noticed the gazes on her, she set her string bass aside and came trotting over.

"Is something the matter, Natsuki?" Midori cocked her head curiously.

"I mean, what's going on with Hazuki? She's been like this ever since the Agata Festival."

Midori slumped bodily at Natsuki's question. Kumiko and Natsuki immediately shared a look upon seeing the obvious gloom in Midori's posture.

Midori fidgeted, clearly reluctant to talk about whatever the problem was, but she finally summoned her willpower and spoke. "I guess...she got turned down."

"Ouch," murmured Natsuki, rolling her eyes. Next to her, Kumiko exhaled softly. Strength seemed to return to her trembling fingertips. So she'd been turned down, had she? Sympathy for Hazuki immediately blossomed within her at the thought. *The poor girl*, she murmured inwardly, the voice in her mind terrifyingly cheerful.

"This is the worst time for complications like that. It's gonna make performing that much harder."

"I tried to cheer her up, but it didn't work at all," said Midori gloomily as Riko and Takuya arrived, carrying their tubas.

"What're you guys doing in a group over there?"

"...Are we not practicing today?"

Natsuki's frown deepened as the pair naturally approached. "Why are couples just as annoying when they work out as when they don't?"

"Aw, Natsuki, don't be mean. I think Gotou and Riko look perfect together." Midori's cheeks reddened and her eyes shone with concentrated sincerity.

Riko rubbed her head self-consciously. "Th-thanks."

"Just make sure you invite me to the wedding!"

Takuya turned beet-red at Midori's wild imaginings. Riko, meanwhile, just smiled uncertainly as she found her usual seat. Takuya sat at a seat near hers and opened his sheet music for the compulsory.

"Hey, now! What're you guys doing all grouped up like that! C'mon, get practicing!" said Asuka as she burst noisily into the room. The third-years' meetings were evidently over.

Wearing a new version of her trademark red-framed glasses, Asuka surveyed the room, her gaze finally landing on Hazuki. "What's wrong?" asked the section leader, but Hazuki merely continued to look out the window.

"She's upset about something, and we were just talking about what it might be," said Natsuki, exasperated.

Evidently Midori was the only one who was truly sympathetic. "Hazuki's been like this for a while, and I'm getting really worried about her! Asuka, is there anything you can do for her?"

A grand smile spread across Asuka's face. "Hmm. To be honest, I don't really care!"

"That's too honest," shot back Kumiko reflexively.

Asuka folded her arms, a frown flickering briefly on her features. "It's true, though. I honestly don't care whether Hazuki plays or not. All I can do is tell her to bounce back as fast as she can."

"Don't be so cold about it, at least! She's a member of the bass section, too, after all!" said Midori.

Asuka replied with a faint smile. "She's gonna wind up in Class B, though, right? What's in it for me if I try to help her out?"

Kumiko gulped at the chill in Asuka's voice. Midori's eyes went wide.

Natsuki's expression remained stern as she controlled herself. "What's in it for you…?"

"Don't you agree, though? Maybe I'd do something if it were going to be a problem for the competition, but why should I help anyone who lets personal problems keep them from practicing?"

"But still—" Midori started to argue, but Natsuki clapped a hand over Midori's mouth, cutting her off.

"Yep, that's right! I say that personal issues should be solved personally!" The ingratiating smile Natsuki forced to her face didn't suit her at all. Midori mumbled something unintelligible.

"Just so long as you understand. Now, all three of you—the audition's coming up, so quit screwing around and get to practice!"

"Y-yes, ma'am!"

"Okay, then. I'm gonna go get my eupho," said Asuka, and she headed for the instrument room as usual.

Making sure the section leader had left, Natsuki exhaled a sigh of relief. Next to her Midori began to flail, struggling to breathe past the hand over her mouth.

"Man, that was scary," said Natsuki.

"Uh, Natsuki, I think Midori's about to suffocate."

Natsuki gasped as she remembered where her hand was and hastily removed it from where it covered Midori's mouth. Freed, Midori took several deep breaths before recovering.

She straightened smartly and glared at Natsuki. "What was *that* for?"

"I mean, I had to do something. You obviously didn't notice how furious Asuka was."

"She was angry?" asked Kumiko.

"Well, not angry, exactly," said Natsuki, glancing at Riko, who was busily staring at her sheet music and pretending not to overhear their conversation. "Asuka, she…she *hates* anything that gets in the way of her practice time. You don't ever want to waste her time."

"But wasn't she kind of mean about it? That was really cold."

"That's how she's always been," said Natsuki with a rueful little smile. Riko and Takuya looked over at her suddenly. A nervous feeling ripped through the classroom, leaving behind a vague unpleasantness that seemed to linger on the tongue.

Natsuki spoke.

"Asuka's…special."

Her voice was the only sound in the silent classroom.

Bored-looking students wearing Kitauji uniforms waited at the otherwise-deserted train station. Kumiko sat on a bench and flipped through a vocabulary notebook. The school had switched to the short-sleeved uniform for the warm season. Kumiko pinched at her upper arm where it emerged from the short sleeve's cuff, sighing. She got the feeling she'd gained weight.

"…Kumiko."

She looked up at the unexpected sound of her name to see a gloomy-faced Hazuki standing in front of her.

Hazuki's schoolbag hung over her shoulder. She tightened her grip on the shoulder strap. "Can we go home together?"

"Oh, sure. Of course."

"Okay," said Hazuki, and sat down on the bench next to Kumiko. Kumiko pointlessly turned the page of her vocabulary notebook.

Apologize: to say you're sorry. Force: to make someone do something. The list of English words floated up in her vision but completely failed to penetrate her mind.

"So I told him how I felt," said Hazuki.

Kumiko looked up from the notebook and over to her friend. *Clack, clack.* The train they were waiting for came gliding up to the platform, but Hazuki didn't move—so neither did Kumiko. The standard phrases announcing the train's arrival echoed across the platform. The doors closed, and the train began to move, leaving just the two of them behind.

"I know," said Kumiko.

Hazuki looked away. "Oh," she said, the corners of her mouth pulling into a slight frown. "I guess there's somebody else Tsukamoto likes."

"...I see." Kumiko frowned. She didn't know the words to respond to that. What were you supposed to say in times like this?

Hazuki looked down. "Sorry."

"For what?"

"That time you tried to help," said Hazuki.

You don't have to tell me. I already know, thought Kumiko, but she said nothing. She flipped through the pages of her vocabulary book. The page with the folded-down corner marked the section that would be on the test. *Apologize. Apologize.* It was the one word she just couldn't seem to memorize, and there were marks all over the margins of that page.

"You don't have anything to apologize for."

"But Kumiko—you like Tsukamoto, right?"

"...Huh?" Kumiko's mouth fell open. What was this girl talking about?

Hazuki took no notice of Kumiko's frozen, wide-eyed state as she falteringly elaborated, as though admitting to some kind of crime.

"I mean, I kinda realized it, but...but I thought if I said something about how I felt first, you might pull back. You're not really the outgoing type, and I...used that. I'm sorry, seriously. I'm...really a terrible friend, aren't I?"

Kumiko scrambled to stop her shame-faced friend from going any further. "Wait, no, hang on—is me liking Shuuichi an established fact?"

"Isn't it?" Hazuki tilted her head in confusion. "I mean, when I took Tsukamoto with me, you seemed pretty upset about it."

"No, but it's not like that with me and Shuuichi at all. Like, we're just…friends? Or something? I think I was just sad at my friend getting dragged away…right?"

"Aha. I see."

"You do? Oh, good."

"Yup, I do. You're totally clueless. Classic."

"Aw, why do you have to be like that?" Kumiko's shoulders went slack.

Hazuki's voice rose in a delighted laugh. It was the first time in days that Kumiko had seen her smile. "You're hopeless! Oh well, the great Hazuki will give you a hand."

"Wait, give me a hand with what? I have nothing but bad feelings about this."

"Oh, you know exactly what I'm talking about."

"No, I honestly do not."

At this, Hazuki stood. Then came the announcement of the next train's arrival. She picked up her bag and smiled—an exhausted, lonely smile.

"Geez, you really are dense."

The train's doors opened. Kumiko hurried to her feet, shoving her vocabulary book back into her bag. Hazuki grabbed Kumiko's arm and pulled her bodily into the train car. Hazuki's hand was warm, but a little bit dry.

Owing, perhaps, to the lingering exhaustion of band activities, as soon as Kumiko arrived home she went to her room and collapsed onto her bed.

"Kumiko, please! Put your lunch box away first!" called her mother from the kitchen, but Kumiko didn't have the energy to respond. She reached over from where she lay on the bed and managed to hit her laptop's power switch.

On her computer were audio recordings of the music Taki had assigned. Kumiko lifted her head up and with some effort clicked the triangular PLAY button. From the computer's speakers came the sound of the compulsory piece. The audition would be very soon.

The band had changed since Taki's arrival. The teachers who'd known the band before all said so. There had been many students who'd complained at Taki's methods early on, but with time they'd stopped. The reason was simple: They could feel themselves improving. Their scattered, messy ensemble performance was steadily coming together and becoming a unified expression of music. It was certainly more fun to participate in a performance that was a source of pride, but music that had been sculpted to the utter extent of their effort was something more than "fun"—it filled their hearts with an emotion that was deeper and more profound than that. Ensemble performance was enjoyable, but it was also intense. To stay on the narrow path they walked, the students had had to sharpen their senses with a new diligence. That was how it felt.

The conductor's job went far beyond waving a baton around during the performance. That was only a small part of his duties. The baton's movements were signals to the players, telling them when to start and stop playing. The conductor had to listen to the sound as a whole and maintain the balance the music required.

Apart from their job during the performance proper, it fell to the conductor to fully understand the composition and the composer's mind alike, and to convey the flow and phrasing of the music to the players. A performance's style and emotion could vary wildly depending on the conductor's choices. Those choices became synonymous with the conductor and defined the reputation of the ensemble. The role of the conductor was far more important than the audience might realize.

Ten years earlier, when Kitauji High School had been a concert band powerhouse, its conductor must have been a talented one. But he'd left the school, and in his absence the band had grown weaker. A simple change in director had made waves that sent the students tumbling. No matter how high their ambitions, without a talented director, they would never win a competition.

Of the over fifteen hundred schools whose concert bands set down the path to Nationals, fewer than thirty would reach their goal. Only three schools out of thirty-six could appear as the Kyoto representatives at the Kansai Regionals. The practice environments of each school were far from equal, with both public and private schools doing their best to perform and win. For Kitauji High School, making it all the way to Nationals was a dream inside another dream.

And yet, Kumiko thought. *And yet Taki is seriously trying to get us there.* The intense practice schedule, the uncompromising rehearsals—they were all for the goal of bringing Kitauji to the National Band Competition. All they could do was give it their best shot.

"…I want to get good," Kumiko murmured.

No one was there to answer.

The auditions would take place over two days. The first day was for brass, and the second for woodwinds and percussion. One by one the students were called to the music room to perform in a small space that had been partitioned off for the occasion. In the hallway outside the music room several chairs were lined up for students awaiting their turn. The classroom was not soundproof, so anyone waiting could hear the playing of the students ahead of them. Just hearing the mellow tone of Asuka's euphonium was enough to send Kumiko's heart racing.

Natsuki slapped the pale-faced Kumiko on her shoulder. "Well, I'm off," she said, and disappeared into the music room.

Her euphonium clasped in her arms, Kumiko simply stared at her sheet music—the places she had to be careful of during ensemble performances, the spots Taki had brought to her attention. She'd gone over the music so many times that the corners of the clear sleeve that held it were thoroughly beaten up. *It will be okay. You can do this.* Kumiko blew air through her instrument and waited for her turn.

"You're up, Kumiko," said Natsuki as she came out of the music room, her own audition over.

Kumiko tried to say something in acknowledgment, but she was too nervous for her voice to work properly.

Natsuki smiled sympathetically at Kumiko's wordless nod. "You, of all people, don't need to be that nervous," she said.

Motivated by her senior's words, Kumiko tremulously stepped into the music room.

"Please, have a seat," came Taki's voice from the other side of the partition. Kumiko wondered if the reason he wasn't meeting them face-to-face was to help the auditioning students feel less nervous, but if anything, she felt even more rattled at not being able to see Taki's face.

There was a seat right in the middle of the partitioned area. She set her clear file on the music stand in front of it and took a deep breath. Her fingers were trembling.

"Please state your name and instrument."

"Ah, first-year, Kumiko Oumae. Bass section, eupho."

"I see," came the curt voice of the assistant director, Michie. So both the director and the assistant director were conducting the test, then. Kumiko took a deep breath to calm her racing heart, opening her stiffened fingers to get them loose.

"Have you done your tuning already?"

"Y-yes, I have."

"I see… Now, Miss Oumae, you have some experience already, don't you? How many years have you been playing euphonium?"

"Um, since fourth grade, so this will be my seventh year."

"Seven years? That's quite something," said Taki in a low, impressed voice. *Crap, I just raised the bar for myself*, Kumiko instantly thought. She shook her head side to side to banish the swirl of negativity. The wooden chair was cold when she sat on it, her sweat-damp thighs sticking to its surface.

"Well, let's have you start with the compulsory, then."

"O-okay."

"I believe the euphoniums come in here, with the secondary melody at bar forty-one. Along with the baritone saxes."

Kumiko hastily looked to her sheet music. Right there—the place she'd practiced over and over.

"I'll start the metronome. Please play until I stop you. You can come in whenever you like."

"U–understood."

Tick, tick, tick. Kumiko took a deep breath as she listened closely to the tempo. She filled her lungs and blew smartly into her mouthpiece. Her fingers moved. Low notes, then high notes. The passage she'd played over and over again during practice. Her sheet music was right in front of her, but she didn't have time to look at it. Her brain shivered with elation. Her breath quavered and her heart flailed like it was about to burst. She thought of nothing, her performance leaping over her consciousness entirely. *What if I make a mistake?* It was a terrifying thought, but there, too, was her joy in playing. A heat arose from her feet to constrict the organs in her chest.

Kumiko played on desperately until Taki spoke.

"Thank you, that's far enough," he said, at which the euphonium's sound came to a sudden halt. Kumiko could hear the sound of something being written down. Was her performance being evaluated in this very moment? The sounds of her playing still lingered, echoing deep in her ears.

"All right. That will do. Please call the tubas in next."

"Ah—yes, sir." Kumiko stood, somehow dizzy. Her hands were still trembling with her nervous energy. She collected her sheet music and fled from the music classroom.

"Ow!"

Her instrument collided roughly with a desk with a loud *ding.* Kumiko frantically checked it, but fortunately the impact didn't seem to have left any noticeable damage. Evidently the audition from a moment ago was still distracting her.

"Are you okay?" asked Midori, peering in her direction.

"Huh?"

"You said 'Ow,' so I thought you'd hurt yourself."

"No, I just banged my instrument."

Despite not sustaining any injury herself, Kumiko would reflexively say "Ouch" when something hit her euphonium. When she explained as much to Midori, Midori smiled cheerfully. "That's 'cause your soul's gone into Jack!"

"Huh? Jack?"

"That's your eupho's name! And by the way, this is George," said Midori, gesturing to her contrabass. Now that she mentioned it, Kumiko did vaguely remember Midori saying something like that back when they'd first chosen instruments.

"Still, Mr. Taki's so mean! Making the contrabass the only one of us that has to audition with the woodwinds."

"Yeah, true."

"I mean, I'm in the bass section, too, y'know?" pouted Midori. There were several Band-Aids on her fingers. Maybe the fancy pink designs on them were Midori's style.

Kumiko squinted and pointed at them. "Are you okay?"

"Oh, these?" Midori smiled. "It happens when you play a string bass. Since you pluck the strings with your fingers, they tend to snap."

"Doesn't that hurt?"

"It does, but not as bad as in middle school!" she said, laughing self-consciously. "In middle school we had a bunch of recitals all on one day, and my fingers were totally torn up after just the morning performances. The Band-Aids kept coming off, and then I'd start bleeding, so when I went to turn my sheet music's pages, I got blood on them. By end of the last afternoon performance, I could barely read my sheet music from all the blood!"

It was all Kumiko could do to smile weakly at Midori's giggling account. That was life at a powerhouse band school for you. Even the little anecdotes were heroic.

"Why'd you keep doing it if it was so tough?"

"Keep doing what?"

"Band. Wouldn't you start to hate it?"

Kumiko asked out of honest curiosity, but Midori shook her head vehemently. The contrabass she held upright with her fingertips was significantly taller than she was. "Nope, that'd never happen. I love band!"

Her voice was so simple and straightforward that Kumiko found herself jealous of the girl in front of her. She wished she could live like that.

★   ★   ★

They had been told that the results of the audition would be announced after final exams. This round of tests would be the second in Kumiko's high school life. She had already stumbled a bit in math, and she wondered if she would be able to get through college entrance exams at this rate. Every time she sat at her desk at home to study, Kumiko wound up worrying about her future.

Extracurricular activities were canceled during the week leading up to final exams, as they had been before the midterms. Kumiko used the time for a change of scenery—a visit to the bookstore. Her textbooks were more than enough study material for the upcoming tests, but she'd been wanting to pick up some new reference books. As her eyes scanned titles like *Pass for Sure!* and *Hit the 90th Percentile!*, it felt like she'd get smarter just by buying one—though any such reference book would immediately become nothing more than a shelf decoration upon purchase, rather than doing anything to improve her grades.

Arriving at the reference section, she saw a section of shelves packed full with red-spined books. On them were printed the names of colleges in big, bold characters. Marveling that so many institutions could actually exist, Kumiko proceeded for no particular reason down the aisle.

"...Hey."

Kumiko quickly turned at the voice behind her. "Aoi?"

"K-Kumiko!" A flustered expression flickered across Aoi's face, but she quickly covered it with a smile, as if to distract from the reference books she was carrying in her arms. The slowness with which she walked toward Kumiko was the proof of how little she actually wanted to have this interaction. "So how's band going?"

"Oh yeah. I'm doing my best. We're off for finals, though."

"Think you'll make it to Nationals?"

"That's the one thing we won't know until it happens."

"Yeah." Aoi narrowed her eyes softly. "...What about Haruka? Is she doing well?"

"Haruka...Oh, you mean President Ogasawara?"

"Yes. I said something mean, after all. Things are kind of weird between us, now."

The "something mean" must have been Aoi's resignation from the band on the day of the meeting.

"She's more or less okay, I think. She's got Asuka backing her up, so."

"Asuka again, huh." Aoi slumped at the mention of the name. "I swear that girl can do everything. She's good at school, she's a great musician..."

"Is she smart?"

"She is insanely smart," Aoi said, then smiled ruefully. Her eyes fell to the reference books in her arms. "My first choice is her safety school."

Kumiko had no idea how to react to that.

Aoi chuckled emptily. "If I were as smart as her, I could've stayed in band." There was an edge to her voice as she spoke. Her tone was light, but in Kumiko's ears it rang with terrible sadness.

"Well, see you," said Aoi as she turned to leave, but Kumiko couldn't help but call out to her.

"Aoi—"

"What?" She looked back.

"Do you regret quitting the band?"

"Nope. Not at all," she said brightly. Her fingers' grip tightened on her arms and left behind red marks on her pale skin, so terrible was her unhappiness.

"Okay," said Kumiko with a smile, and she pretended to believe her.

4 ♭Good-Bye, Competition♪

Notwithstanding the shudders that came with the return of her scores, Kumiko made it through test season in one piece. Her math grades continued to fall, but on her way to the music classroom where the band director awaited, she told herself with completely unfounded optimism that she'd figure something out. The members of the Class A ensemble would be announced today. Tomorrow, meanwhile, would see the assignment of first and second parts within the various sections, as well as the announcement of the soloists.

"Wonder what's gonna happen with the bass section," said Midori, stroking her chin with a serious expression on her face. "My gut says everybody's gonna pass! 'Cause we don't have very many members to begin with."

"…I hope so." Kumiko sighed softly. In one corner of the classroom was an expressionless Reina, and across from her to the right was Shuuichi, fooling around with some of the boys from the percussion section. First-, second-, and third-year students alike wore equally tense expressions. Well, except for Midori, who seemed fine.

"I'm the only one on string bass, so I pretty sure I won't fail," said Midori with a smile, as though she'd read Kumiko's mind. She probably wouldn't miss her guess, either. Her playing was excellent, and there wasn't anyone else in the band who could handle a contrabass.

The classroom door slid briskly open, and an energetic voice filled the space. "Is everyone here?" said Michie as she strode in. She wore a stiff black suit that didn't seem appropriate for the season at all. There was no Taki behind her. Evidently the assistant director would be delivering the audition results.

"All seventy-one of the students who auditioned are present," said Ogasawara.

"I see," replied Michie, setting a file on top of the room's piano. "Moving right along, I'll be announcing the Class A band members. Anyone whose name isn't called will be participating in Class B ensemble practice, which will meet in AV Room Two."

"Yes, ma'am!"

"There will be fifty-five students in Class A. When your name is called, answer promptly and loudly."

"Yes, ma'am!"

"Furthermore, there will be no objections raised regarding our decisions. The band members were chosen without bias or favor. Bear that in mind. Is this understood?"

"Yes, ma'am!"

"Good," she said, and opened her file.

Kumiko wondered what it was about being faced with this teacher that made her sit up straighter. Something told her that everyone's responses would be louder than usual.

"I'll begin with the trumpet section."

With these words a hush fell over the classroom. The quiet tension could have been mistaken for calm. There were eight students in the trumpet section who'd auditioned: two third-years, three second-years, and three first-years. Some of them would certainly be headed for Class B. Kumiko gulped and watched Michie's face. The teacher's expression was unreadable.

"Third-year, Kaori Nakaseko."

"Here!"

"Third-year, Sana Kasano."

"Here!"

"Second-year, Yuuko Yoshikawa."

"Here!"

"Second-year, Junichi Takino."

"Here!"

"First-year, Reina Kousaka."

"Here!"

"That concludes the five assignments for the trumpet positions."

The moment Michie said so, a second-year student's hands went to her face in surprise. The sound of a girl's weeping quietly filled in the classroom. Nobody was pleased. Nobody said congratulations. The atmosphere was obviously wrong for that. The air was damp and close. Tension weighed on Kumiko's shoulders. She wanted to get the announcements over with and get out of this place. She wanted to escape. She looked down, then stole a glance at Reina. Reina was sitting ramrod straight with her eyes fixed on Michie.

"Next, the horn section. Third-year—"

Michie's voice continued to call out names. The named students, when called, stifled their happiness and responded with stern expressions. Some of the students cried when they were passed over, while others bore it in silence.

When the trombones' turn came, Kumiko discreetly glanced over at Shuuichi. His eyes were tightly shut as though he was praying, but when his name was called a smile split his face. His right arm wavered, almost wandering about in the air. Was he trying to find some way to express his feelings? Failing to find anyone to share his triumph with, he quietly rested his arm on the desk in front of him. Then, seeming to suddenly notice Kumiko's look, he met her gaze.

Congratulations. She tried to somehow convey it with her eyes, but it didn't seem to reach him. He gave her an awkward look, then quickly turned away.

"Next, the bass section. Beginning with the euphoniums."

The bass section's turn had come. Kumiko swallowed and clenched her fists. Her heart pounded. *It's all right. There are only three euphoniums. The chances that one of us will get dropped to Class B are low.* As Kumiko frantically tried to calm herself, Michie began to speak.

"Third-year, Asuka Tanaka."

"Here." Next to Kumiko, Asuka's voice rang out, calm and brimming with confidence. And surely she had been confident. Confident that her name would be called.

"First-year, Kumiko Oumae."

"Wha…" Kumiko stumbled over her reply, thinking she'd misheard. But no—Michie had said it. "First-year." It couldn't be. A terrible shiver ran down her spine, a cold sweat dampening her back. She felt impaled on the dubious looks directed at her.

Michie made a strange face. "Oumae! Your answer!"

"H-here…" she finally managed. The insides of her clenched fists were wet.

"That concludes the two assignments for the euphonium positions."

Michie's voice continued on ahead. Takuya, Riko, Sapphire. All the members of the bass section after the euphoniums had their names called. *Except for—except for—* Her mind churned. Rationality crumbled like paper in flame, flooding her brain with memories of the past.

*

"G-good morning!"

Kumiko gave her usual morning greeting but did not receive the usual response. Her senior took her eupho out of its case. Her silver euphonium. There were two silver euphoniums in Kumiko's middle school band. Obviously the golden instruments were cool, but Kumiko preferred silver. It felt like there was something special about them.

"Um…hello?" Kumiko addressed the other girl, who radiated hostility but said nothing. They were the only two people in the silent instrument storage room. Kumiko had only just entered middle school and still felt thoroughly uncomfortable in the space. The other girl waited for Kumiko to finish taking out her instrument as Kumiko wondered if she was ever going to say anything. The storage room was small, so normally students had to leave the room

before taking instruments out of their cases. But since the girl had
left her instrument case wide open in the middle of the music classroom, Kumiko hadn't been able to put away her own case.

"Hey."

"Y-yes?" Kumiko's voice cracked at being suddenly addressed. She
looked to see the older girl glaring at her. She instinctively backed
away at the hostility.

This kind of nonnegotiable hierarchy was the most terrifying part
of middle school. Despite the small difference between the students'
ages, the older ones strode around the school like they owned it.

"Are you making fun of me?"

"Huh? Wh-what do you mean?"

"I'm asking you if you're making fun of me." The girl's glare was relent-
less in the face of Kumiko's denial. She made a disgusted tongue-cluck
at the silent Kumiko. She reached out and seized Kumiko's wrist, nails
digging into skin. "You think you're above me now that you're in A?"

"N-no, I don't—"

"Yeah, you do. Pretty full of yourself for a first-year!"

The girl kicked at Kumiko's euphonium. The brass instrument with
its flaking silver plating clattered to the floor. *Ouch!* Kumiko thought.
Her vision blurred. Her precious instrument had been damaged. What
if it had been dented? What if it was broken? The recital was so soon.

"If it weren't for you, I'd've been in A."

"I'm…I didn't…"

"Shut up. I don't want to hear it," the girl had said, flinging
Kumiko's hand away with enough force to knock her to the ground.
Her elbow struck first, and Kumiko's hand went instantly numb.
The older girl gazed coldly down at the crumpled Kumiko.

"You're nothing special," she spat. The words pierced Kumiko's
heart. The weight of accumulated sobs made it impossible for
Kumiko to speak. The older girl snorted derisively and left the room.

Even after she made sure the girl was out of sight, Kumiko's
hands wouldn't stop shaking. She frantically rubbed the place on
her wrist where she'd been grabbed. The friction warmed her skin,
but the marks didn't fade. She dropped her gaze and saw her fallen

euphonium looking defenselessly up at her. As she cautiously reached for it, she saw her face reflected in its silver surface.

*

In the end, that girl had graduated without Kumiko ever really getting to know her. For her, that competition would have been her final performance in middle school. But Kumiko, a brand-new first-year student, had unforgivably stolen her seat. She'd always been nice to Kumiko up until that day, but that had changed overnight, and from then on she ignored Kumiko entirely. The mood in bass section continued to be unpleasantly awkward until she graduated, and Kumiko had considered quitting the band several times. But she couldn't do it—she couldn't summon the courage to say, "I quit." That year, Kitachu won the silver prize at the Kansai Regionals.

The girl's eyes that day—Kumiko would never forget them. Kumiko loved music. She loved her instrument. But she didn't love the school band. She knew perfectly well the ugly feelings that lurked behind the smiling faces of so many of the people involved in the band. She couldn't trust them. She would never have Midori's honest, innocent love for the band.

"The aforementioned fifty-five students will perform in Class A. I expect Mr. Taki's instruction will be even more intense now, so I expect those of you who were chosen to rise to the occasion."

"Yes, ma'am!"

Michie's words brought Kumiko back to the present with a start. The announcement of band member assignments was apparently over, and the assistant director was calmly putting her file back in order. The mood in the classroom remained gloomy.

"Soloists and part assignments will be announced tomorrow. Those of you for whom part assignments are not relevant should attend your regular sectional practice."

"Yes, ma'am!"

"That's all for today's meeting. Don't dawdle on your way home. Dismissed!"

"Thank you very much!"

The band members all echoed the president's words. Michie favored them with a satisfied smile, then strode out of the classroom. The students began gathering their things to leave, complicated expressions on their faces.

There were those who had been chosen, and those who had not. In that moment, a clear division had been drawn between the two groups. Kumiko sighed as she packed her things into her bag. Her nervous sweat had turned cold.

"What, you're going home already?" Kumiko felt something hit her back. She looked up. The arm over her shoulder felt heavy.

"N-Natsuki..." Recognizing the face behind the voice, Kumiko paled. Memories from middle school flashed through her mind. The sweat from her forehead dripped down the side of her face toward the floor. "Um, look, I..."

The words caught in her throat. She winced. Her heartbeat roared in her ears. Despite the dizzying heat that gathered at Kumiko's face, Natsuki's arm seemed somehow chilly.

"What're you freaking out for? What's with the face?" said Natsuki with a laugh, flicking Kumiko's forehead.

Kumiko unconsciously covered the spot with her hand. "Um, what are you doing?"

"Hm? Nothing special, really," said Natsuki as she took Kumiko's arm. She was strong, but not like the older girl from middle school. It was a comforting strength. "Hey, are you doing anything after this?"

"I don't really have plans..."

Natsuki's expression was open and friendly. "Great. Let's go to McD's."

"Mac's?" *Sure*, Kumiko was about to finish, but Natsuki snorted in sudden laughter.

"'Mac's'? A Mac is a computer."

"Yeah, but I mean...it's Mac's."

"Where's that 'a' sound coming from? It's obviously McD's."

There were all kinds of contractions and nicknames for things that were different in the Kansai region than they were in the Kanto Japanese that Kumiko spoke. The intonation and pronunciation could also differ, and Kumiko frequently found herself dragged into debates about them midconversation. Eventually someone would realize they'd abandoned whatever the conversation's original topic had been and put an end to the trifling digression.

"Anyway! Let's both of us go to McD's. I'll treat you if you stay under a hundred yen."

"What can you even get for a hundred yen? And also, it's Mac's."

"You can get stuff! McD's is a student-friendly establishment," said Natsuki with a smirk.

The nearby fast-food joint was full of students wearing familiar uniforms. Natsuki secured the table in the farthest corner with practiced ease and set her things down on the bench side like she owned the place. This resulted in Kumiko sitting in the chair across from her.

"So what do you want?"

"Er, I...guess I'll have a shake."

"Roger that." Natsuki gave Kumiko's shoulder a light pat and headed for the register. Kumiko wondered if she should let Natsuki act like a junior student being ordered around by a senior, but then she looked at their bags in front of her and realized it would be a bad idea to leave them unattended. She sat quietly and waited for Natsuki's return.

"Strawberry okay?"

"Oh, anything's fine!"

"I mean, I'd make you drink it even if you said you hated it. I'm on team chocolate, myself," said Natsuki when she returned, offering Kumiko one of the cups on the tray she held.

Kumiko hesitantly took the cup, a bright red straw already sticking out of its top. Natsuki flopped grandly down on the bench side and sighed noisily. "Man, I didn't get picked!"

"*Koff!*" Kumiko had nearly forgotten about the situation, and when it was thrust back in front of her, she choked on her shake.

Natsuki watched Kumiko and cackled. "Aw, were you trying to be nice about it?"

"N–no, I mean..."

Kumiko hadn't been trying to be nice. She wordlessly stirred her straw around in her shake. It was just that she hated that Natsuki hadn't been picked for Class A.

"Don't worry about it. I mean, when you think about it, it's not surprising at all. I only started band in high school, so I've only had a year on the eupho. Obviously you'd be the pick."

"But…"

"And it's not like this is the last year we're gonna go to a competition, anyway. I'll just have to work hard to make Class A next year," said Natsuki, taking a sip of her shake, flattening the yellow straw between her lips.

"…You're a good person."

Many thoughts were running through Kumiko's mind, but that hackneyed phrase was the one that she spoke aloud.

Natsuki's eyes widened for a moment, but then she collapsed into delighted laugher. The straw that dropped from her mouth had bite marks on it.

"No, no, no, you've got it all wrong."

"But you're being so kind to me about all this!"

"That's just because you're being so thoughtful it kinda made me feel bad for you!" Natsuki continued. "Look, to be honest I don't really care about the competitions. A or B, whatever."

"Huh?"

"That kind of thing just seems like a pain, you know? I'll do it if everybody else is doing it, but still," Natsuki said with a shrug, "the reason I joined this club in the first place is because I heard you could slack off. It's only this year that everybody's gotten all fired up. I just can't keep up with the change."

Natsuki looked away and brushed condensation from her cup's surface with her fingertip. Kumiko quietly sipped her shake, its artificial sweetness sticking to her tongue.

"Do you know about how our club did in competition last year?"

"Bronze prize at the All-Kyoto Competition, right?"

"Yup. Kyoto doesn't have district competitions, so we were basically the worst."

Gold prize, silver prize, bronze prize—competition participants were divided into those three categories. The high school bands competed over two days, and the schools that would advance to the Kansai Regionals were chosen from among the gold prize winners. Larger prefectures would have district competitions before the prefectural level, but Kyoto didn't.

"The truth is, there were some kids last year who wanted to shoot for the gold prize. Nobody thought we could go to Nationals, though."

"...And they were the second-years I keep hearing about, who all quit?"

"Yup," nodded Natsuki. "I mean, I was just a first-year. But they tried to convince the seniors to work harder, practice more."

"They sound pretty amazing."

"It was wasted effort, though."

Wasted. Kumiko repeated the word inwardly. She didn't like the sound of it.

In front of her, Natsuki's lips curved into a derisive sneer. "The upperclassmen crushed them, after all."

"Crushed... Do you mean...?" Kumiko paled.

Natsuki shook her head. "Oh, they didn't bully them or anything. They just ignored 'em. Everybody just pretended the people who wanted to work harder didn't exist."

"...Uh, doesn't that count as bullying?"

"Maybe, but they sure didn't think of themselves as bullies. They were just ignoring something they thought was annoying."

"Still..."

Natsuki laughed at Kumiko's frown. "Of course, there were some of the seniors who practiced a lot, like Asuka. But she only plays for herself, so she wasn't any help."

"What do you mean?"

"I mean exactly that. Asuka's happy as long as she can play her own instrument. She doesn't care if the rest of the band sucks, or whether they win a competition. Everybody around her was slacking off, but she was practicing like crazy. That's why she's so good."

It was true that Asuka's skill set her apart from the rest of the band.

Taki had probably chosen the compulsory piece that emphasized the bass section based on Asuka's euphonium and Midori's contrabass skill.

"Asuka's neutrality is scary. She didn't support *anybody*. Both the kids who wanted to practice more and the ones who wanted to screw around tried to get her to come around. 'Asuka's special,' everybody said. But in the end she wouldn't get behind anybody. She's always neutral. The other seniors, the older students—nobody had any concrete complaints they could make about her. So finally the ones who wanted to work harder just quit. Kitauji got bronze, but nobody cared, because they'd given up."

Asuka's special. Natsuki had said so over and over again.

"Aoi worried about the girls who quit, though. President Ogasawara, too. When the seniors graduated and Ogasawara took over as club president, the mood in the band got a lot better. And then Mr. Taki came...heck, plenty of the third-years now were always working hard even before, and now we've got some first-years with experience at Kansai and even Nationals, so overall we're way better. Heck, we're even considering going to Nationals ourselves. It's crazy. But...I guess Aoi just couldn't forgive herself."

—They've got no right to tell me, "Well, I'm gonna work hard!"

Aoi's words from before momentarily filled Kumiko's ears. Her eyes had been colored with anguish in that moment.

"...So, Natsuki, were you...were you friends with any of the second-years who quit?"

"Why would you think so?"

"Well, I mean...you sound kind of angry."

"Angry...at who?"

"At the third-years who graduated last year, or...everybody who pretended nothing was happening."

Natsuki let a small chuckle slip at Kumiko's question. She fingered her straw and stirred the thick contents of her cup. She licked clean a bit of shake that lingered on her lips and gave Kumiko a significant look. Her red tongue peeked out past her slightly parted lips. "Why do you think nobody was willing to work hard for last year's competition?"

"Huh?"

"I mean, sure, Mr. Taki's scary and all, but that's not really a reason to push yourself. Last year there were plenty of us who thought anybody who wanted to work hard was a weirdo. But this year we've got people crying because they didn't make the A band. Isn't that kind of freakish? Doesn't it make you wonder what the problem was up until now?"

"That's…yeah, I guess."

It did feel a little too sudden for a simple change of heart. The band had been terrible and lazy at the entrance ceremony. What had changed them? Kumiko had only started at Kitauji this year, so she didn't know how true everything Natsuki was saying was. But it was certain that the band had changed profoundly this year.

"It's the mood."

"Sorry?" Kumiko blurted out at the sudden statement.

Natsuki narrowed her eyes and repeated herself. "Like I said, it's the mood. Our little band is really susceptible to the mood in the room. So when everybody's like, 'Let's work hard,' they do, but when they're like, 'Let's not bother,' they don't. I think that's the only difference between this year and last year. Nobody knows who they really are."

The final sentence slipped from Natsuki's lips. It seemed directed at somebody else, Kumiko thought—or maybe at Natsuki herself.

"So in that sense, Mr. Taki's really good at getting everybody on board. At creating that mood."

"That's probably true."

"Right?" Natsuki grinned, satisfied at Kumiko's response. "Like at that first ensemble practice. Wouldn't it have been easier if he hadn't stopped us halfway through, and then just given us a lot of advice and stuff? Nobody would've wanted to go against him if he'd just done that. He's good at it."

"I guess so."

"But that's not what Mr. Taki did. I think he wanted to make a point from the very start."

"Make what point?" Kumiko frowned.

Natsuki's lips curled into an unpleasant smile. "About just how terrible we really were."

Kumiko reflexively gulped.

"He's an amazing strategist. Everybody was way better by just the second ensemble practice. That's thanks to his teaching. The improvement forced us all to acknowledge his ability. Mr. Taki is a guy who really knows how to use mood."

"Mood, huh," murmured Kumiko.

Natsuki nodded firmly. "In the end, we just got caught up in the mood. That's all," she murmured, almost as though talking to herself.

Kumiko crumpled up a few paper napkins into a ball. The mangled wad rolled listlessly across the table. The straw in her hand was the bland, tasteless color of blood.

With final exams, Kumiko faced her second academic counseling week. Her previous session had been a three-person meeting including her mother, but this time it was just Kumiko and her homeroom teacher, Michie. When the assistant band director saw Kumiko's face, her expression softened.

"So, are you working hard in the concert band, Oumae?"

"Ah, yes," said Kumiko, withering. Michie was famously stern with groups of students, but one-on-one, she was distinctly more gentle. This transformation was surely part of why students both feared and adored her.

"Have you gotten used to high school?"

"I think so, pretty much," said Kumiko with an honest nod. Seeing her from this close, Kumiko could see the many wrinkles that lined Michie's face.

"You were chosen for the Class A performance, weren't you?"

"Y-yes, that's right."

"Are you nervous?"

"I am. But I'm used to that."

"I see. That's promising," said Michie, her eyes narrowing slightly in a smile. Outside the window, the cicadas buzzed away. It felt like the sun-melted summer itself was sticking to the window's glass.

"Are you having any problems, as a student?"

"Maybe...my math test grades."

"That's certainly a problem. Make sure you review properly," said Michie with a little chuckle.

"Yes, ma'am." Kumiko nodded her assent, absentmindedly playing with her bangs.

"Have you given much thought to your academic future? What career you'd like to pursue? Your dreams?"

"No, not really."

"I see. Well, there's plenty of time in high school. No need to rush your decision."

"Yes, I guess not."

"But do make sure you study your math. If you keep putting it off, you could wind up too far behind to improve your grades at the end."

"Y-you're right about that."

"So long as you understand," said Michie, patting Kumiko's shoulder. Her hand was finely lined with wrinkles. Blue veins stood clearly out beneath her pale skin. Kumiko found the sight vaguely disquieting. She realized that Michie was around the same age as her own mother. Such were the vague thoughts that occupied her mind.

Her counseling appointment concluded, Kumiko headed to band practice. Just walking through the halls, she could hear the sounds of other students practicing. She listened closely.

"...We really have gotten better," she murmured.

Compared to when she'd first heard the band, the individual playing skills were much improved. Which was unsurprising given the amount of fundamentals practice they'd all done. Still, considering how well even the first-years were able to play through their music, as she admired the achievement, she felt a certain unease tugging at the corners of her heart—was she herself really good enough? She worried about being overtaken and left behind. Kumiko took deep breaths to keep the feeling of unworthiness at bay, her expanding lungs forcing her other organs aside.

As she approached the music room, she heard the sounds of some kind of commotion coming from inside. She hastily checked her watch.

Strange—sectional practice should still have been going on. And then she remembered that today was the announcement of the soloists.

The instrument storage room was connected to the music class-room. There were already several students huddled in the storage room, all of them focused intently on whatever was happening in the classroom.

"You wanna watch, too?" said one of the percussion seniors, ges-turing her over. Unable to refuse, Kumiko found herself joining in and peering through the cracked door. There were still quite a few students in the classroom. Trumpets, flutes, horns, oboes...all sec-tions with soloists.

"I cannot accept this!" A shrill voice pierced Kumiko's ear, and she winced. "Why did they pick Kousaka instead of Kaori?"

It was Yuuko, the trumpet player, who was exploding in anger. Next to her, Kaori smiled nervously. "Well, but they chose Reina after the audition, so..."

"I don't accept that!" Yuuko stomped a foot. The students around them exchanged glances and whispers. "It is sort of weird for a first-year to get the solo, isn't it?" "Shouldn't it have been Kaori?" "She should've read the room and turned it down." The murmuring voices were all talking about Reina. But as Reina gathered her sheet music into her folder, she seemed not the slightest bit concerned.

"Come on, let's try to calm down..." Ogasawara patted Yuuko's shoulder, but Yuuko brushed her roughly away and glared at Reina.

"Hey, you! Stop ignoring me!" Yuuko grabbed Reina's arm force-fully. Reina's music file slipped from her hand to the floor.

"...What do you want?" said Reina. Her insolent tone only made the atmosphere in the room more threatening.

"Don't give me that! I want to know why you got picked for the solo instead of Kaori!"

"Yuuko, that's enough," said Kaori, trying to hold her back. But Yuuko would not be stopped.

Reina looked over the senior band member in front of her. Her lips suddenly parted as she spoke. "What do you mean, 'why'? You know perfectly well why."

"What—"

"I'm the soloist because I'm a better player than Kaori is. Simple, isn't it?" spat Reina.

Rage colored Yuuko's cheeks. Kaori, who had frantically been trying to calm Yuuko down, now froze in shock. A skim of tears brimmed in her big eyes.

"...Is that really the only reason?" said Yuuko.

"What are you trying to say?" shot back Reina, narrowing her eyes. Her freezing gaze made Kumiko want to run. Her soft gasp wasn't the only one.

"You knew Mr. Taki from before he was a teacher here, didn't you?"

Reina's eyes went wide. Her ever-neutral expression now betrayed astonishment for the first time. "Wh-why does that matter all of a sudden?"

"I heard your dad is friends with Mr. Taki. That's why he's playing favorites—"

"Don't you dare insult him!"

The instant the words "playing favorites" came out of Yuuko's mouth, Reina's cheeks flushed red. With her free left hand she slapped Yuuko's grip off her arm. The *smack* sound echoed hollowly in the room. Kumiko had never heard Reina say anything with that much emotion.

"I don't care what you say about me, but don't drag Mr. Taki into this! I can't believe you're insulting our director like this right before a competition! Do you really think he would play favorites?"

Yuuko gulped, silenced by the intensity of Reina's words. Ogasawara was no help at all as she looked to and fro uncertainly. *If only Asuka were here,* Kumiko thought, biting her lip. The timing of the vice president's guidance counseling appointment had been terrible.

Kaori's voice trembled. "R-Reina, I'm really sorry! She's just trying to stick up for me—"

"Kaori!"

"Yuuko, you have to stop saying that kind of stuff, too. I really don't mind—" Kaori started to speak, but then, strangely, she paused. It was as though whatever had been holding her emotions back had broken, and tears spilled from her eyes. They reached her cheeks and slid down her smooth skin. Kumiko could tell the entire classroom had fallen silent.

Kaori wiped her eyes with a fingertip and forced a shaky smile to her face. "It's…really okay." Her voice shook.

Sympathetic murmurs rippled through the classroom.

"She really shouldn't have talked that way to a third-year." "Kousaka's so nasty. Poor Kaori." "Does Kousaka really need to play the solo? Shouldn't a senior get to play it?"

Reina faced the rising voices of discontent with a sharp glare. The open emotion she'd shown a moment earlier was gone. After removing all feeling from her expression, she looked over the room. Her brows furrowed slightly.

"If you want to complain, do it after you're better than me," spat Reina, and she left the music classroom. Kumiko gulped as she saw the way Reina's fist was clenched. Just because she wasn't letting it show on her face didn't mean she hadn't been hurt.

"Reina!" Before she could think better of it, Kumiko began to chase after her.

"Reina! Reina!"

Kumiko frantically ran after her. The sight of someone running through the halls like that drew curious glances from the other students as she passed them, but Kumiko didn't care. Reina didn't look back as she stubbornly walked on ahead. It was as though she was trying to get away from Kumiko.

"Wait, please!" Kumiko soon found herself out of breath, her lack of exercise catching up to her. She had confidence in her lung capacity, but she was on the wrong side of the athletic ability curve. She was only able to finally catch hold of Reina's arm because Reina had stopped walking.

"Waugh!" Kumiko cried out as her head painfully rammed into Reina's back. It hurt.

Reina said nothing as Kumiko rubbed her head. She just stood there. They'd made it all the way into the interior of the school building. In front of them was the staircase leading to the roof. There were no other students.

"...Um, Reina...?" said Kumiko hesitantly, still holding on to Reina's wrist. The black-haired girl remained silent, glaring at the floor, her jaw set. From between her lips emerged a low sound. "...ll..."

"Huh?" Kumiko reflexively asked.

This time Reina spoke clearly, her eyes flashing open. "I can't stand them! I can't stand them! *God*, I hate them! What the *hell* is their problem? Why is everyone being so shitty about this! Ugh, it pisses me off so bad! They're so annoying!"

The girl's shouts echoed in the hallway. She was so suddenly loud that all Kumiko could do was blink. Reina's expression turned relieved, and she exhaled a deep sigh. Her hand was at her chest. She slowly moved it to grasp Kumiko's.

"Why are you making that face?" Reina smiled.

"I mean, I thought you were sad."

"I'm not sad. I'm pissed off," said Reina with a quick smirk.

Kumiko's chest tightened at the obviously false expression. *You don't have to smile*, she thought.

Reina continued to look wordlessly at Kumiko, and after a few moments had passed, she slid her hand down along Kumiko's arm. Reina's pale skin seemed unreasonably hot. Kumiko looked down. Sweat from the sides of her face rolled down to her collarbone. She brought Kumiko's hand up to brush against her red-flushed cheeks.

"Kumiko..." was all Reina said before embracing her bodily. Kumiko was instantly flustered by the soft sensation of the other girl's body through her clothes. Reina clasped her arms around Kumiko's back and hugged her tightly. Hesitantly, Kumiko returned the embrace.

"Kumiko," repeated Reina. Her voice was despondent, and Kumiko gently stroked her delicate back. She could feel Reina's spine underneath her uniform. As she slowly traced along its length, her fingers caught on the band of Reina's bra.

"Do you think I'm wrong?"

"No, I don't."

"Really?"

"Really."

"Okay. Okay," said Reina, burying her face in Kumiko's shoulder. Kumiko could see Reina's long, straight fall of hair. There in the shadowed corner, there was nothing to illuminate her.

The two stayed there like that for a while, until Reina, seemingly satisfied, released her embrace. She scratched her cheek self-consciously, then sat down on the steps.

"C'mon," said Reina as though it was obvious, and Kumiko complied, sitting beside her. She accidentally stepped on Reina's skirt, but she didn't seem to mind. Kumiko noticed Reina's pale thighs emerging from under the navy-blue fabric.

"Hey, um…would you mind listening to me for a little while?"

"Can I even refuse?"

"No, but still." Reina let a smile slip and leaned against Kumiko. She was mundanely heavy. "My dad's a professional trumpet player."

"Whoa, really? That's amazing."

"Yeah, that's my dad," said Reina with a little laugh. "He's been friends with Mr. Taki's dad for a long time."

"Mr. Taki's dad?"

"Yup. Tooru Taki—he's a really famous concert band conductor. He got gold at Nationals over and over."

"Wow, was Mr. Taki's dad really that amazing?"

"He was. When I was little, it was my dream to be his student someday." Reina looked down, lost in the memory. "But he was pretty old, and he retired before I started high school."

"Oh, so then…"

"Yup. When Tooru retired, I decided I wanted to study under his son, our Mr. Taki. That's why I came to this school."

The long-standing mystery of why Reina had chosen Kitauji was finally solved. But there were still questions remaining. Kumiko tilted her head. "But how did you know Mr. Taki would be at Kitauji? He just started this year."

"I leaned on my mom a little bit for that. This is just between you and me, but I actually knew he'd be coming here before he did."

"Okay, that's just scary." Kumiko regarded Reina's mysterious smile and decided not to ask any more questions. Reina giggled happily, then suddenly straightened and looked up at Kumiko. Her eyes sparkled as though filled with scattered stars. Still holding Kumiko's hand, she squeezed it tight.

"The thing is, I like Mr. Taki."

"...Huh?"

"Oh, but not just 'like.' I mean *like* like. Love."

That's the worse of the two likes, Kumiko vaguely thought to herself as she regarded the suddenly bashful girl. But they said love knows no ages, so maybe even if he was a decade or more older than her, it would be okay.

Reina's eyes faintly narrowed. Her pale lips curved. "That's why I can't let anything happen to his reputation because of me."

Her voice was low, but it carried in the quiet space. Kumiko looked up to the end of the stairs. The doors at the top leading to the roof were chained shut, as if to prevent anyone from flying too high.

"...Do you think you might give the solo up to Kaori?"

"No," came the immediate answer.

"You're gonna hear about it from everyone," Kumiko said.

This prompted a snort from Reina. She folded her arms and smirked, undefeated. "I'll show them I'm right, then."

Kumiko couldn't help but let slip an impressed "Ooh" at Reina's righteous declaration. Her words stood on a foundation of absolute confidence in her abilities, something Kumiko herself utterly lacked. Reina seemed to shine, and Kumiko found herself averting her eyes. "Yeah. I bet you will," she said with a soft smile.

Reina's eyes narrowed in a smile, and she stood, taking Kumiko's hand. The soft palm of her hand was shockingly cold.

Kumiko parted ways with Reina and returned to the music classroom. Few students remained, with just the percussion section conducting their normal practice. She wondered if Reina would go to trumpet sectionals. Yuuko would definitely be there, and Kaori, too. Kumiko was impressed all over again at Reina's stout heart.

She picked up her euphonium and made her way back along the

hallway, when suddenly she heard a voice from above. When she looked up, she realized the voices were coming from the landing at the top of the stairs that led to the next floor. It was Kaori and Asuka.

"So I hear there was some kind of crazy fight, huh?"

"Yuuko, she kinda...yeah."

"Well, she really likes you, after all."

"Yeah, it's nice, but...it can be a problem, sometimes."

At this Asuka loosed a loud cackle, eliciting a sulky "Geez!" from Kaori. "It's not funny!"

"Ah, sorry, sorry. So how's the mood in the trumpet section now?"

"It's horrible. Reina came to practice as usual, but Yuuko's still furious."

"I just wish she could give it a rest for now, with the competition coming up. I don't want the trumpet section splitting the band."

"...Sorry."

"Well, it's not your fault, Kaori." Asuka chuckled. "It's rough being so popular."

Kaori sighed. When she spoke, her voice was lowered and wetly hoarse. "...Asuka—"

"Hm?"

Kumiko suddenly wondered if this conversation was something she shouldn't have been listening in on. But her interest had been piqued, and she couldn't very well leave now.

"Asuka, who do you think should do it?"

"What, the solo?"

"Yeah," Kaori nodded, her voice soft and muffled.

"I think whoever's better should do it. Seems like that's the standard Mr. Taki is using, anyway," said Asuka.

Asuka's answer was logically sound. Kaori's voice choked up as she replied. "So you're saying Reina's better?"

"That's not for me to decide."

"Now you're just dodging." Kumiko heard the sound of a soft impact, as though Kaori had jokingly smacked Asuka. "I don't want you to say it, even if you're kidding."

"Say what?"

"...that Reina's better than me."

"I never said any such thing. You're the one saying that," Asuka spurted.

Unable to argue with that, Kaori murmured some kind of hasty response. The conversation seemed to have turned sweetly sentimental. Kumiko made a face, when suddenly a voice called out to her from behind.

"Kumiko, what're you doing here?"

"Yeep!" Startled, she turned around to see Hazuki, carrying her tuba. "N-nothing!"

"Oh, really? Well, whatever." Whether or not she was actually curious, Hazuki didn't pry further. "C'mon, let's go," she said.

At her suggestion, Kumiko headed with her to the classroom where their sectional practice was held. Despite listening carefully, she caught no more of her seniors' private conversation.

The closing ceremonies for the first semester concluded without incident, and Kitauji High School officially began its summer vacation. On the school grounds and in the gymnasium, the various athletics clubs devoted themselves to training in anticipation of the summer tournaments. It was intensely stifling to hear their bellowing voices in the hallways and courtyard.

Concert band practice entered its final spurt, becoming even more intense. Weekend practice was normally from nine AM to five PM, but it was extended to eight PM, with the approaching competition being given as the reason. The band members cried and wailed at the never-ending rehearsals and practice. After playing the music for their performance so many times, the melodies began to etch themselves into the students' consciousnesses. Kumiko began to find herself a little frightened as she caught herself humming the music in the bath or in bed as she fell asleep.

"So, the schedule for the competition day has been announced," Taki said with a smile one day after they'd finished fundamental drills and tuning. The band's eyes were all instantly on the director.

The Kyoto Concert Band Competition was held over two days. For Class A, roughly thirty bands would perform on August fifth, with the remaining ten or so playing on August sixth. Only the top three among them would advance to the Kansai Regionals. The order of performances was decided by lottery, but this luck of the draw could sometimes have a significant effect, despite its slight unfairness. An earlier number meant less time to practice. It wouldn't make or break a band's chances of success, though.

"Kitauji High School will perform at eleven AM on the second day, following Rikka High School."

A groan of dismay arose from the band at this information. Playing after a known powerhouse school meant they would inevitably be compared directly to it. This order was hardly fortuitous for them.

"It will be all right." Taki smiled. "Few bands have chosen 'Crescent Moon Dance' as their compulsory piece, and our free piece will not overlap, either. I'm sure that the judges will hear our performance with fresh ears. Additionally, I don't believe that Kitauji's playing will fail to measure up to Rikka's."

The band members' eyes all brightened at the director's words. Having become thoroughly used to his constant criticism and scolding, they were awfully susceptible to any praise from Mr. Taki.

The judges would decide the outcome of the competition. Their job was not an easy one. They heard the same pieces of music over and over again, which evidently became tiresome. There were five pieces of compulsory music to choose from, but owing to the pieces' varying degrees of difficulty, certain compositions were often predominant. Sometimes a popular choice would be performed ten times in a row by different schools, so it might work to Kitauji's advantage to have chosen a less-common selection.

"Incidentally, Rikka's compulsory will be 'March for Military Band,' and their free is 'Music of the Spheres.'"

At this there were cries of despair. Philip Sparke's "Music of the Spheres" was well known as a difficult piece. A few years earlier, a high school from Fukuoka prefecture had won national acclaim with a performance of the notorious piece that put even professional bands to shame. Kumiko had gotten a recording of it from her middle school band director and listened to it over and over. Rikka was well known for their marching skill, but they were strong in concert performance as well. They'd surely be able to pull off even a difficult piece.

Taki smiled sympathetically. "There's no need to be afraid. We will be fine performing the music we've prepared. Results are proportional to effort, and I know how hard you've all worked."

"Mr. Taki!" a high voice cried out. Something was strange about him today. He'd been nothing but complimentary. For just a moment, his gaze met the skeptical-looking Kumiko's. Her heart thudded at his clear eyes. His smile in that moment was full of implications, but then he looked ahead to the classroom in general.

"Now then, we'll begin rehearsal. First, a complete run-through."

The band instantly straightened at the sight of Taki's raised baton. Kumiko readied her euphonium and set its mouthpiece against her lips.

By the time practice was over, the once-bustling school buildings had fallen quiet. By eight o'clock, all the other students had gone home, and the campus became dark and gloomy. The halls were deserted. Only the green-glowing emergency exit signs illuminated the dark, silent space. The shadows that fell in the hallways were unpleasantly creepy, and Kumiko started at even slight noises.

"Ugh…"

Why did she have to accidentally leave her wallet in the sectionals practice room? Kumiko cursed her own absentmindedness as she walked. Fortunately, there was still a light on in the staff room. Maybe one of the teachers was still working. She wanted to borrow a key and get her wallet as soon as she could. Summoning her resolve, Kumiko slipped into the staff room.

"Excuse me…" she said.

The faculty had mostly gone home, and the staff room was much dimmer than it usually was. Fluorescent lights lit just one corner of the spacious room. Who was still here? As she swept her gaze over the room searching for a person, the scent of coffee tickled her nose.

"What might you be doing?"

Kumiko turned around to see Taki, holding a mug in his hand and regarding her with a look of surprise. White steam rose from the orange mug.

"It's eight thirty—a bit late for students to be wandering around, I think."

"Ur, um—I left my wallet in my sectionals room…"

Taki sighed, mildly exasperated. "You're a euphonium, correct, Miss Oumae? Do you practice in classroom three-three?"

"Th-that's right."

"Understood. I'll accompany you. Let's be brisk about it." He set his mug on his desk and took the classroom key from where it hung on the wall.

"I-is that okay?"

"Excuse me?"

"Um, I mean, you going along with me."

Taki cocked his head curiously. "Did you want to go alone?"

"No, no, it's just…you seemed busy with work."

"Oh, that's fine. I was just doing some preparation for tomorrow's rehearsal," he said with a friendly smile. Why was this Taki so different from the one who held their rehearsals? Kumiko couldn't help but wonder. He was a gentle soul—until music got involved.

The two of them, Taki and Kumiko, walked down the silent halls. This was the first time she had ever talked to him like this, Kumiko realized as she silently followed the director.

"Are you enjoying concert band?" Taki suddenly asked her, jolting her out of her reverie.

"Y-yes!"

"I see. That's good to hear. The truth is, I got a bit of a scolding from the principal about how I'm making you all practice too much."

"Really?"

"Really. I was reminded that the third-year students have entrance exams, and that I shouldn't push them too hard," he said. "But I'm not too worried about it," he added.

Be a little *worried about it!* Kumiko thought, but she said nothing—Mr. Taki was an authority figure, after all.

"Make sure that you don't neglect your studies, either, Miss Oumae."

"I-I will."

"Still, I was abominable at chemistry when I was in high school, so I suppose I can't say too much."

The pair's footsteps echoed through the quiet hallway. The mostly unlit school was dark enough that you couldn't see to the end of the hall.

Kumiko's mouth was dry. She looked up to Taki's face as though to beat down the vague unease that rose within her.

"Mr. Taki, do you really think we can make it to Nationals?"

She seemed to have caught him with his guard down. Taki froze briefly in place. "Miss Oumae, you don't mean to tell me that you think we can't make it, surely."

"N-no, it's not that. Just…"

"It's no good to lose heart now. You must be undaunted in all things." Taki began walking again.

Kumiko hurried to follow, musing to herself that Taki wasn't very quick on the uptake. She wondered if that was something Reina liked.

When they reached the room, Taki produced the key and slid it into the keyhole. He turned it, producing a mechanical *click*. "There, it's open."

"Th-thank you very much!" Kumiko quickly turned on the lights. Her wallet was right on the desk where she'd left it. She hurried over to retrieve it. "I found it. Sorry to bother you!"

"No, it's no trouble." He didn't seem the least bit concerned as he locked the classroom back up again.

As Kumiko gazed vacantly at his long fingers fluidly turning the key, a question popped into her head, and she suddenly asked it. "Mr. Taki—how did you become a band teacher?"

"Are you really that curious?" Taki's eyebrows drooped in exasperation, and his cheeks faintly colored. It was rare to see this sort of reaction from him.

Kumiko's curiosity was now intensely piqued, and she nodded firmly. "Yes!"

Taki seemed to consider it for a moment, then finally shrugged and gave in. "My father was a concert band teacher. It was probably his influence."

"Your father—that's Tooru Taki, right?"

"My, you're well informed," said Taki with a look of surprise.

"I heard from Reina," said Kumiko, looking down.

"Ah, that's right. You're good friends with her, aren't you?"

"Ah, yes. We are quite friendly."

Taki chuckled, apparently finding Kumiko's statement amusing. "My father was the concert band director here ten years or so ago, so I was quite pleased to be assigned here myself."

"Really?" This was news to Kumiko.

"Really." Taki nodded with a happy smile. Had the golden age of concert band at Kitauji High School been Taki's father's doing?

"Did you always want to be a teacher?" Kumiko asked.

Taki smiled softly. "No, not at all. I was a child with all sorts of dreams—I would read a comic book and announce that I wanted to become a comic book artist, then watch a movie and want to become a film director or actor. I think I wanted to do pottery at some point, even."

"That's...that's really something."

"However," said Taki, giving Kumiko a significant look. "However, in the end, this is the work I chose."

"...Do you regret it?"

"That's a good question." His chuckle echoed down the hallway.

Kumiko suddenly realized that he only ever seemed to smile.

"Thank you very much, Mr. Taki." Kumiko made sure to properly express her appreciation as soon as they returned to the staff room.

"Not at all," replied Taki with a little nod. Kumiko wondered if the cooling coffee on his desk would wait for him. "It's quite late. Take care on your way home."

"Yes, sir." Kumiko nodded, holding her schoolbag. She'd put her wallet deep in the innermost pocket, the better to avoid losing it.

"Oh, Miss Oumae."

"Yes?"

Kumiko had almost left the room when Taki called out to her. She looked back and saw him regarding her with a serious expression. Right there was the only bright place in the entire darkened school. The glow of the cheap fluorescent lights stretched weakly out through the staff room's windows. Taki stood there as though treading on the shadows. His usually gentle eyes now suddenly burned with a keen brightness. "I do believe that this band can go to Nationals. I believe so very seriously."

Kumiko held her breath. She instantly understood that this was the answer to her question earlier. He believed in them. The idea filled her chest with warmth. Her throat caught on something. She took the happy, embarrassed feeling she had and flung it back at Taki. "I'll…I'll do my best at the competition!"

Witnessing this artless expression of emotion, the director silently showed her a wide smile.

With each moment the competition drew nearer, the mood in the band grew tenser. It was surprising how thoroughly they'd learned the compulsory piece, given how impossible it had seemed at first. Their rehearsals grew more and more polished, and as the days went by, Taki's instruction shifted from the basics of rhythm and pitch to higher-level guidance on nuances of expression. As the students applied their best efforts to taking Taki's words and making them reality, their passion compounded their labor. And while it would be easy to see this and imagine that the club was unified, there were some who intensified their opposition in order to resist the trend.

"The sheet music says *affettuoso*, so why are you playing the melody like you're grumbling? Let's try to play it more smoothly." Taki flipped irritably through the score.

"Yes, sir!" replied the trumpet section he'd addressed. Their reply was quick and attentive, but exhaustion was written all over their faces, which was hardly surprising. This was the thirteenth time they'd played through this section at Taki's direction. Kumiko was getting tired of just hearing it, never mind playing it.

"We'll do this as many times as it takes," said Taki with a pre-emptive smile, as though having read the band's mind. The trumpet section scrutinized their sheet music, scared into submission.

"Now, then, trumpets and percussion, one more time."

"Yes, sir!"

Kumiko could not hear any difference between the fourteenth version of the section and the thirteen that had come before it, but Taki evidently could. It was heartening to have a band director whose ear was so finely attuned to the smallest disparity in sound, but when it was your own performance being scrutinized, it was simply terrifying.

"That's enough. Let's try playing it one by one. Starting with Miss Nakaseko."

"Yes, sir."

At Taki's direction, each member of the trumpet section played through the section individually.

"Miss Kousaka, would you please play it again? I believe your F was a bit sharp."

Taki's correction elicited nasty giggles from around the room. Reina remained expressionless, simply answering, "Yes, sir," and playing the phrase again.

"That level right there is about acceptable," said Taki. "Next, Miss Yoshikawa."

Taki's instruction had moved onto the next student, but the laugher from a moment earlier lingered in Kumiko's ears and refused to fade. Since the day of the audition, the rift between Reina and the older students had only deepened. The maelstrom of ill feelings was pulling other students in and disturbing the overall mood of the club. With the seniors supporting Kaori and the juniors backing Reina, the only thing stopping the situation from exploding might be the shared goal of the competition. And if that was so, what would happen after the competition was over?

Kumiko mulled the situation over as she polished her instrument with a cloth.

"All right, now everybody together, one more time."

"Yes, sir!" replied the members of the desperate, exhausted band.

★   ★   ★

"Ugh, this sucks!" cursed an irritated Hazuki, not even bothering to hide her ill temper.

"You mean the thing with Kaori?" replied Midori innocently, eliciting a flinch from Kumiko at her willingness to plunge directly into the sensitive subject. Kumiko glanced around warily, but it looked like the rest of the band members had already gone home and weren't lingering at school. She slumped as they continued on down the road that led away from Kitauji.

"What do you think, Midori?" asked Hazuki.

"About what? Whether I'm on Kaori's side, or Kousaka's, you mean?"

"No, obviously you gotta pull for Kousaka. I mean, I like Kaori, but I sure don't like the girls around her," said Hazuki, displeased.

"I dunno, I mean, I kinda get it. It'd be super annoying to have a younger student steal the solo out from under you. It's gonna be Kaori's last competition and all."

"Don't tell me you're on Kaori's side!"

Midori shook her head vehemently at Hazuki's question. "No, no. I want to do well in competition, so I totally think Kousaka should do it. There aren't many students as good as she is even at the national level. But, like..." Midori trailed off and heaved a sigh.

"But?" Kumiko prompted.

"But I wonder if that's all that matters."

"What do you mean?"

"I think there are things that matter besides competition results. It seems kinda sad to just decide everything by skill," Midori explained, her long eyelashes lowered as she looked down. Kumiko quietly encouraged her to continue. "We got the gold prize all three years I was in middle school. Seijo's an all-girls school, and there was drama like this all the time. Everybody fought over stuff like auditions, who was gonna be in the A band, all that stuff. Juniors would get totally ignored by the seniors, or juniors would badmouth the seniors. I mean, we still basically all got along, but still."

"Ugh, that sounds like the worst," said Hazuki, scowling.

"But that's when I started thinking, what if I hadn't gone to that school—what if I'd gone to a school that only ever got as far as regional competitions, and we all just aimed for a gold prize there and kinda just took it easy? We might never make it to Nationals, but I bet it would still be pretty fun."

"So you're saying that competition results aren't everything?"

At Kumiko's question, Midori folded her arms and thought for a moment, then nodded lightly. The cat keychain attached to her schoolbag bounced with the movement. "Yeah! I think that's pretty much it," she said with a smile.

Hazuki gave her an exasperated look. "That's fine and all, but I don't think a nice sentiment's gonna be enough to fix this. People want results."

"I think we could still aim pretty high even with Kaori doing the solo, though. To be honest, Kaori's really good. It's just that Kousaka's abnormally good."

"So you really do think Kaori should play the solo, then."

"I mean, if she did, then all this fighting we're having now would go away! And Kousaka can play the solo next year."

"But wouldn't you feel bad for Kousaka, then? She'd be giving up the solo to someone who's not as good as she is."

"But I hate that kind of thinking!" said Midori. "Sometimes it's okay to just give it to somebody who tried really hard!"

"Well, if that's what it's about, then Kousaka's been practicing like crazy, too."

"Yeah, but she's the reason everybody's fighting now."

"But that's not *her* fault!"

"I know, but there's no other way to fix it!"

Midori and Hazuki normally got along very well, but they tended to argue about the most trivial things. As the one to whom it fell to break them up, Kumiko found it intensely frustrating.

"What do you think, Kumiko?"

"Yeah! Kumiko, what's your take?"

Midori's and Hazuki's voices overlapped, and Kumiko's face involuntarily twitched. In times like these, it was better not to endorse either position. Her eyes wandered here and there as she tried to think of a way to change the subject—and then someone entered her field of vision.

"Hey—" she said.

The two other girls followed her gaze. There, coming out of the convenience store next to the station entrance, was Shuuichi. As soon as he caught sight of them, he visibly winced.

"Oh, it's Tsukamoto," said Hazuki. "Heey!" she called, waving him over. As far as Kumiko knew, he'd rejected her just two months earlier, but it didn't seem to be bothering her.

As soon as he spotted Kumiko, he ducked back into the convenience store as though trying to escape. She was aware that he'd been avoiding her, but to see it happening so obviously was irksome.

"Eep, Kumiko, you're making a scary face!" said Midori in delight, poking Kumiko between her eyebrows. It hurt a little.

Next to Midori, Hazuki snorted. "That awkward weirdo."

"Ooh, Hazuki, your face is nasty, too!" cried Midori, clearly happy for some reason as she continued to poke at Kumiko's face.

Kumiko smacked her hand away, then exhaled in relief. Midori's treatment was irritating, but it didn't really matter if the subject stayed changed.

"Thank you very much!" The band members all bowed. For once, the day's band practice had ended before the sun went down. The reason was simple: Taki was out on a school-related trip. It was the first time in quite a while she was off by midday, and Kumiko walked along the school hallway in pleasantly high spirits.

"Hey, Kumiko. Good work today!" Reina approached, having already finished getting ready to leave the school.

"You going home?" asked Kumiko.

"Yeah. What about you?"

"I'm gonna stay a little longer."

"Okay. See you tomorrow!"

"See you!"

Reina smiled and waved, and Kumiko returned the gesture. As soon as Reina was out of sight, the senior students all around them immediately began whispering. "She's going home already?" "She shouldn't be leaving ahead of her seniors." "The competition's so soon—she's sure taking it easy."

The unpleasant murmurs seemed to cling to Kumiko's ears. She pretended not to hear them and hurried toward an unoccupied classroom. She wanted to get away as quickly as possible. Lately it was always like this. No matter where Reina went, criticism seemed to follow. One more thing to endure until the competition was over.

Kitauji High School's southern building had four floors, and climbing to the top one was an exertion. Kumiko usually practiced in the north building, but she'd wound up here in an effort to find someplace thoroughly deserted to practice. The southern building's fourth floor was notably unpopular, which made it perfect for solo practice sessions.

"...Huh?"

As she climbed the stairs, Kumiko stopped when she heard the notes of a familiar musical phrase. It was a trumpet's soft tone—the solo section of the free performance.

Hiding herself behind the corner, Kumiko peered down the hallway. Evidently someone had gotten here first. Kumiko's favorite practice spot was already occupied by Kaori, looking at her sheet music as she played. Her posture was straight, and Kumiko realized that Kaori must have completely memorized the solo; her eyes were not actually on the music, but looking somewhere far in the distance.

"Why is she...?" Kumiko murmured to herself—but just then, someone tapped her on the shoulder.

Kumiko gasped and turned to see a smiling Asuka, carrying two plastic drink bottles and holding her index finger to her lips in a *shh* gesture. She gestured silently to Kumiko to follow. Kumiko stared blankly at Asuka as the girl descended the steps, then came to her senses and hastily followed.

"You saw, eh?" Asuka asked with a mischievous smile once they'd reached the third floor.

Flustered, Kumiko stumbled over her reply. "I-I'm sorry! Should I not have?"

Asuka giggled. "Just kidding," she said, sitting down on the stairs. Kumiko wondered if the drink bottles Asuka was carrying were for Kaori. She wondered if the two of them were going to practice together.

"So why are you here, Kumiko?"

"I was going to practice here…"

"By yourself? Ah, sorry we took your spot," said Asuka, but she didn't seem particularly sorry. The older girl's hair was tied back, and she yawned. "Are you surprised?"

"Huh?"

"By Kaori, I mean. She's been privately practicing the solo. That's a secret, by the way." Asuka narrowed her eyes slightly. Behind her glasses' lenses, her eyes betrayed no emotion.

"So Kaori, she…"

"She doesn't want to give up, looks like."

"I…I see." Kumiko looked down at her feet, unable to hold Asuka's gaze any longer. With nowhere to go, her bewildered euphonium leaned against her.

"So Kumiko, you're friends with Kousaka, right?"

"Ah, yes…"

"Is that why you're making that weird face? Don't worry, Kousaka's gonna be the soloist anyway," said Asuka, her voice sounding as though she didn't care what happened one way or the other.

"B-but…"

"I mean, Kaori knows that Kousaka's better, too. But she doesn't want to give up. C'mon, let the girl practice."

"No, I'm not criticizing her or anything, I just…"

"Heh-heh. Is it sympathy, then? 'Aw, poor Kaori…'"

There was a palpable edge to Asuka's voice now. Kumiko gulped. Asuka took one of the plastic bottles and twisted the cap off. She swirled its liquid contents around. Light reflected off the water's transparent surface.

"The people around her don't quite understand. Kaori doesn't want sympathy, and she doesn't want to argue her way into getting the solo. She just wants to be satisfied."

"Satisfied?"

"Yup," said Asuka, taking a drink of water. Her throat bobbed as she swallowed. Kumiko inwardly debated whether to ask the question, and after a few moments, she finally spoke.

"...So are you on Kaori's side?"

Asuka stopped drinking. The moment she took the bottle from her mouth, droplets of water made dark spots on the floor. She forcefully wiped her mouth with the back of her hand and smiled a wry, troubled smile. "Why would you ask me something like that?"

"Natsuki said that you were 'special.' I just thought that was a little weird. I thought you'd be neutral, as usual."

"Yeah, that girl overthinks about me sometimes."

"Really?"

"Yup. Still, she's not exactly wrong."

"What do you mean?" Kumiko tilted her head, and Asuka giggled.

"I'm not especially on Kaori's side, but I'm not on Kousaka's, either. I'm the vice president, after all. It wouldn't be appropriate for me to express my personal opinion like that," said Asuka, standing. Kumiko wondered if that meant the conversation was over.

"Okay, then, but...I'll keep it a secret, so please just tell me."

"What?"

"Your personal opinion."

Asuka's eyes widened for just a moment—she seemed not to have expected Kumiko to go that far. But the expression of surprise was soon swallowed by her usual smirk, and she answered with an amused, throaty chuckle. She touched her index finger to her bright red lips. "Can you keep a secret?"

"I-I'll try."

"At least you're honest."

The plastic bottle in Asuka's hand sloshed. On the water's transparent surface, foam appeared, then vanished. Her long eyelashes swept up and down. Her obsidian eyes suddenly focused on Kumiko.

"To be honest, in my heart of hearts, I don't care. I don't care about who plays the solo or any of the rest of that crap."

The chill in her voice froze Kumiko to the ground where she stood. Asuka noticed this reaction; the corners of her mouth curled up into a smile. She patted Kumiko's shoulder, then nudged her back slightly, as though sending her on her way.

Her fingers, much longer than Kumiko's own, fluttered through the air as she waved. Kumiko doubted she could ask any more questions of that tightly closed mouth.

Kumiko smiled wordlessly. Asuka said, "Bye-bye," as she disappeared back up the stairs, presumably to where Kaori was.

Kumiko watched her go before moving. She descended the deserted stairs. She still wanted to put the question to Asuka's smiling face: *You actually want to cheer Kaori on, don't you?* But she couldn't. She wasn't strong enough to peel that sturdy mask from Asuka's face.

Kumiko sighed. Even now, she could hear the faint voice of a trumpet lingering in her ears and refusing to fade.

It was the day before the competition. The band had reserved a small performance space in the neighborhood for the day's rehearsal to practice the performance, as well as entering and exiting the stage. The municipal concert hall near Mt. Oubaku charged a very reasonable rental fee and thus became a great ally of band students.

"Sh-shuddup!" cried Hazuki, covering her ears. The Class B band in which she played would have its competition performance two days after the A band, on August eighth. Their duties today involved helping the A band with transporting their instruments—as well as appreciating their performance. She'd worn a simple jersey shirt today, perhaps to make the physical activity easier, and as the wail of a siren sounded within the hall, she looked exhausted.

"You mustn't tell the band to shut up. Although it is pretty loud," said Riko from behind Hazuki with an exasperated smile.

At the moment, the percussion section was putting the final touches on its performance. The instrument with the most impact in "East Coast Pictures" had to be the siren that sounded during the finale. Many schools settled for using a siren whistle for the piece, but Taki had gone to the trouble of borrowing a hand-cranked emergency siren from another school. According to him, its sound had a different weight. Given how loud it was, no mistakes could be made in its playing. The terrible weight of this responsibility fell to a first-year percussion student, who looked about to cry under Taki's instruction.

"Hey, Kumiko—don't get nervous and screw up, okay?" said Asuka with a malicious grin from where she sat next to Kumiko.

As she applied oil to her instrument's valves, Kumiko nodded, her face obediently serious. "I-I'll do what I can!"

"Even I'm getting excited! I can't believe tomorrow's the real thing!" chattered Midori, seemingly delighted. Midori really was tough as nails. She seemed utterly ready for the performance and untouched by anything like stage fright.

"Well, it's not like you have a solo or anything to worry about. Let's just try to have a good time," said Natsuki, looking to Kumiko with a grin.

Behind Kumiko, Takuya nodded. "...We'll do our best."

"We will!"

It was still just a rehearsal, but Kumiko felt somehow heartened nonetheless. She responded to Takuya with admirable energy.

When she looked around at the other sections, they were all busily engaged in their own crucial practice. The instruments' melodies mixed in the air, each one a grain that formed part of a huge, complicated, swelling din. It might have sounded like a tremendous noise to an outsider, but strangely, those swept up within it felt nothing of the sort.

Only the hall's stage was lit, and there were only a few audience members in the seats. Given how nervous Kumiko felt in the modest hall, she imagined that it would be much worse at the actual event. She had never been much good with crucial performances. Her brain went blank with nerves.

The competition was held every year at the Kyoto Kaikan concert hall, which was in the city of Kyoto proper. It was a large venue, and on the days of the event it would be swarming with students. The competition performances might have already started there; it was the first day of the All-Kyoto Concert Band Competition. Which bands had already scored well? Kumiko felt strangely ambivalent; she both did and did not want to know.

"Good. All right, everybody, let's do a full run-through, with the percussion." Taki stepped up to the conductor's lectern, apparently satisfied with the state of the siren. At the sound of his voice, everyone scurried to their places, and the clamor from a moment earlier vanished as though it had never been, leaving the hall quiet. The almost painful silence bore down on Kumiko's shoulders.

"Um—!"

Suddenly there was a raised hand at the edge of the hall. The soft voice was a familiar one.

"What is it, Miss Nakaseko?" Taki's eyes fixed on Kaori.

"I would like to redo the audition for the solo section," said Kaori.

At these words a loud murmur rippled instantly through the band. The sheer timing of the request was incredible. Kumiko drew a sharp breath and looked to Reina. Her expression was as unreadable as it ever was, but her fingers trembled a bit, holding her sheet music.

"We only have the use of this hall for a limited time. We don't have enough time to test all of the members of the trumpet section again."

Yuuko bolted to her feet. "I withdraw! I have no desire to play the solo."

Following her lead, the other second- and third-year trumpets also stood. Reina did not move. She stared at her sheet music as though to hide her dismay. Taki looked down, considering the possibility. Finally he took a deep breath, exhaling it in a sigh. The moment he cast his gaze back over the band, the murmuring instantly evaporated into silence.

"Understood. Very well. We will now hold another audition for Miss Nakaseko and Miss Kousaka to decide the trumpet soloist. Will that do?"

"Yes, sir!" Kaori nodded fiercely in response to the director's question.

The cornet solo was indisputably the highlight of the second movement of "East Coast Pictures." The beautiful tune pulled behind it a grand melody. It was more relaxed than the third movement, which only further emphasized the passage's beauty. Sloppy technique would not suffice.

"We'll begin with Miss Nakaseko. Everyone who comes in at the top, please make sure to play. Is that understood?"

"Yes, sir."

Taki brought his baton down. Kaori's soft, delicate playing filled the hall. She performed everything perfectly—including the difficult high notes, and the tricky passages where each note had to be smoothly connected to the next. There wasn't a single fault in her bright, sparkling tone. Kumiko closed her eyes and let it flow over her. Kaori's performance had noticeably improved. It spoke clearly of the exhausting effort she'd put into it.

Taki smiled when the performance was over. "You've certainly improved. I'm impressed."

Kaori's tense expression immediately brightened, and the students around her burst into spontaneous applause. Kumiko looked to Reina. It would be hard to follow this. Reina placed her hand to her chest and took a deep breath. For the first time, the obvious fact of Reina's own nervousness occurred to Kumiko.

"Now then, it is Miss Kousaka's turn. Are you ready?"

"Yes, sir."

Reina readied the cornet. Her back was ramrod straight; her gaze, directly ahead. Taki brought his baton up, and Reina took a breath.

From the moment the first note leaped from the trumpet's bell, Kumiko clearly heard the difference between this and the performance that had just ended. The shock seemed to strike her brain. The high notes stirred the air and penetrated deep into Kumiko's ears. Reina's tone was forceful while still preserving its beauty as it reached to the end of the concert hall. The same sheet music ought to produce the same sound—but the two performances were undeniably different. Kumiko swallowed reflexively at the thrilling, electric sound. Her heart thudded; goose bumps stood up on her skin. The smooth melody seemed to have no seams at all between its notes, and passion suffused the sound.

The performance ended, and silence fell in its wake. No one moved. No one spoke. Traces of what they'd just heard still lingered in the air.

This...this isn't fair, thought Kumiko. *How can someone like that be my classmate?*

"Thank you very much," said Taki.

At this, Reina lowered her instrument. The band members came out of their reverie and began to murmur, giving their thoughts on the performances as though they'd forgotten they were in the middle of ensemble practice. Every face seemed flushed with excitement.

"Quiet, please!" Taki clapped his hands. The chattering students finally fell silent. Taki wrote something on his score, then finally looked to Kaori. He smiled, and spoke.

"Miss Nakaseko, would you like to play the solo?"

Kumiko heard held breaths from all around. Reina's eyes went wide, her pain obvious on her face. Her pupils strained. Surely Taki could hear it, too. There was an insurmountable wall between Reina and Kaori. Kumiko glared at Taki with all the protest she could muster. Taki's countenance, however, never changed. He continued to regard Kaori with that kind, gentle expression.

After several seconds of silence, she answered. "No." She looked down, and tears fell from her eyes. "...I can't."

Reina looked up in surprise. Kaori regarded the junior trumpet evenly, and even Reina, surprisingly, shook away at her gaze.

"I think you should play the solo." Kaori's voice quivered, and her eyes were red. She gave voice to her true thoughts, surely, but her expression spoke of emotions that were very different. The trumpet in her hand sparkled innocently.

Reina closed her mouth and dipped her head forward in a short bow, her black hair rippling. "I'm sorry I was so full of myself, before."

Next to her, Yuuko's eyes widened. Kaori looked down. "It's okay. It was true, after all." Her voice was so serious that Kumiko had to look away.

She just wants to be satisfied. Asuka's words suddenly echoed in Kumiko's ears, and for the first time she understood them. Kaori had probably known the truth all along—that her playing wouldn't measure up to Reina's. But she didn't want to give up. She wanted to truly lose. To have the overwhelming difference show. To have her heart broken. She had practiced a solo she would never perform, over and over, just so she'd be able to accept her loss.

"Miss Kousaka," Taki said, carefully articulating her name.

"Yes," answered Reina, her face still stiff.

"You will play the solo. Not Miss Nakaseko. You."

Kumiko saw Reina's finger twitch. The gentle curve of her back straightened. "Yes," she said again, her voice ready and confident.

Taki smiled gently, then looked nonchalantly down at his score. "Now then, back to the subject at hand. Let's play it from the top."

The ensemble practice began again in earnest.

"You mean you *don't* hate it?" Reina had asked after their final middle school competition. She was normally so collected, but in that one moment, she had betrayed her feelings. Kumiko had wordlessly looked on, unable to do anything else as Reina sobbed.

In middle school, Kumiko had chosen concert band out of something like inertia. She wasn't particularly athletic, nor did she have any other serious interests. She'd become used to having her hands on an instrument and was frightened of severing her connection to music—so she'd chosen concert band. She'd done her best, practicewise, but also hadn't been especially serious about it. She mostly did it because everybody around her was doing the same thing. Her place in the concert band wasn't so desperately important to her that she wouldn't be able to quit even if the seniors started shunning her. She was just afraid of losing it. That was all.

Reina had cried, but Kumiko had not. She simply wasn't very attached to the outcome. She hadn't worked terribly hard for it. She hadn't come to a place that demanded her tears. And while Reina sobbed, Kumiko had looked away, because she had realized that truth. That this was her final competition in middle school—and still. And still.

She hadn't regretted the outcome at all.

This was their last stage rehearsal, Taki had said. The members of the Class B band sat in the audience seats of the little hall, their attention on the stage. The spotlights were bright white. In the thoroughly air-conditioned hall, the stage was the one hot place.

"Let's perform as though this is the competition itself."

"Yes, sir!"

Backstage, Michie held a stopwatch. Kumiko clung to her golden euphonium and took a deep breath. Her lungs inflated, then deflated as she exhaled.

"The Kitauji Prefectural High School Concert Band," said Michie in place of a proper announcer. The students all moved immediately, walking to their standby locations. Kumiko sat in her seat, steadying her euphonium on her lap.

Taki readied his baton. Kumiko watched him. She heard the sound of a breath. There was a moment's stillness—then, as if to shatter it, the trumpets' melody. Then, layered above it, the flutes' melody and the solo came in. The tubas' thick sound shook the air. The euphs would be coming in soon. Along with Asuka, Kumiko readied her still-silent instrument.

With her breath came the sound. Pressing the valves down changed the sound. It was so simple, yet such a delight. And so difficult. Her eyes on the baton, Kumiko desperately followed the music. The clarinets and flutes ran throughout the score, tearing through their phrases with terrific speed. The oboes' and bassoons' counterpoint. The melody moved from the woodwinds to the brass, then back to the woodwinds. The soul of the sound contracted, then expanded, again and again, charging toward the climax. Atop the French horns' brilliant tone and the forceful refrain of the euphoniums and trombones, the trumpets sent their melody soaring. A sudden crescendo. The band's volume reached a peak, then slammed to a finish.

The sound of the compulsory piece still echoing, the band members turned their attention to the free performance.

In the silence, first the trombone harmony sounded out, joined by a clear, high flute solo. Following it, the cornet solo began. The music flowed. It was gentle, the beautiful tones melting into the air. Then, as if to add just a bit of color, the euphoniums added their timbre. The sounds layered, and layered again, gradually building in energy. They came to a grand, final crescendo, then plunged ahead into the third movement.

The movement began with a magnificent brass melody, accompanied by runs from the woodwinds. It was lively music, a deliberate contrast with the compulsory piece's obscure, hard-to-grasp melodies. Here, the melody danced from section to section, constantly moving. Each grain of sound sparkled, the rhythm light, sprightly.

Then the raucous melody suddenly fell silent, and the hall was filled with a leisurely, flowing sound, its phrases harmonious and beautiful. Then—interrupting it, a piercing siren. The peace of a moment earlier vanished, and sound flooded the hall again. With the end in sight, the band's performance grew feverish. The music accelerated, the sound suffused with urgency. The band held the swell and pushed through to the end of the score. The performance hit its ultimate climax just as Taki's baton signaled the final note.

"...Perfect," Taki said.

A compliment like this from Taki was completely unprecedented, and the students looked at each other in surprise. Before them, the members of the Class B band were standing and applauding. Kumiko, too, believed that it had been a perfect performance. It felt so good. There hadn't been a single mistake. A fresh, light sensation unlike anything she'd experienced before ran down her back. *This is fun*, she thought. *Playing this music is so much fun!*

"Let's play tomorrow just like we played today. We will be fine. You can do this," said Taki, setting the baton down on the music stand. His gaze swept across the faces of the whole band. "We will absolutely go to Nationals."

There was confidence in his voice, and a corner of his mouth pulled up in a daring smirk.

It would be great to go to Nationals. Kumiko had often thought as much, ever since middle school. But it had only ever been so much lip service, and she'd never actually believed it could happen. Expectations invited humiliation. It was the height of stupidity to have a dream that could never come true. She'd always felt that way.

But an unspoken wish could never become reality.

Kitauji High School was absolutely going to Nationals. Kumiko made a fist as though to strengthen her resolve.

"Yes, sir!" There beneath the white-hot spotlights, the students' energetic voices rang out.

It was the day of the competition. The band boarded the bus, each of them wearing their school uniform and a serious expression. Kumiko and the rest of the band had assembled early that morning for one last run-through in the music classroom. They'd then packed their instruments up in their cases and made one final check to make sure nobody had forgotten anything. Since the percussion instruments were both very heavy and very particular about how they preferred to be carried, loading everything up had taken some time.

On way to the SunFest, the bus's cabin had been cacophonous, but today it was excessively quiet. A few students even looked downright ill from nerves.

"Hey, look! I spotted another four-leaf clover taxi! That means everything's gonna go great today!" Next to Kumiko, Midori gazed out the window innocently. She giggled. "I can't wait to perform. I was so excited last night I didn't sleep at all! This is gonna be great!"

"...Midori, you are incredible."

"Huh? What do you mean?"

"Oh, all sorts of things."

Midori tilted her head curiously at Kumiko. Her expression was entirely normal, without so much as a hint of nerves. As she gazed at the girl's face, Midori suddenly reached out and pinched Kumiko's cheek.

"Kumiko, don't tell me, are you nervous?"

"Noh ah alhh!"

"Wow, you are such a liar!" said Midori, releasing Kumiko's cheek. Thanks to hauling that giant contrabass around, she was surprisingly strong. Kumiko rubbed her still-throbbing cheek and regarded Midori.

Midori noticed her gaze and grinned in response. "Listen, the reason you're nervous is because you're thinking you don't wanna mess up. You gotta stop thinking like that, and start thinking like, 'Gaze upon my flawless technique!'"

"...Midori, is that what you're thinking when you play?"

"You betcha! I'm supergood, so I want lots of compliments from lots of people!"

"I...I see."

"Yeah!" Midori smiled, carefree. Kumiko couldn't help but be a little envious of her ability to brag so easily.

Midori laughed, then set about humming the compulsory piece. Her songbird-like voice followed the part of the contrabass. Kumiko joined in, humming the euphonium part. Singing the bass parts, the two of them could not complete the song's body, but behind them Asuka began to sing out loudly as well. Kaori grinned wryly and started singing the trumpet part. Once a pair of third-year students began to sing as well, the whole band rapidly joined in, each singing out their own parts. At first they were hesitant, but then their voices grew louder and more confident, a grand chorus in the bus. They sang the compulsory, then the free, then the compulsory, over and over, not stopping until the bus reached its destination.

After unloading their instruments from the moving truck, the band quickly set about preparing for their performance. Kumiko opened the case and took her old friend out. Polished with a cloth, the euphonium sparkled with the color of the sunlight that bathed it. Kumiko realized that she'd been with the euphonium ever since fourth grade. Seven years. Seven years, she'd lived with this instrument.

When she'd first heard its name, it had struck her as a rather dull instrument. It seemed kind of plain. And it was obscure. It didn't look cool at all. But Kumiko had grown to like the euphonium. It was plain and obscure, but its sound was warm and beautiful. She had often wanted to switch to a different instrument, but in the end, she had been the one who chose the eupho. Kumiko liked the euphonium. She didn't just like it. She loved it. And she had just realized it for the first time.

"Have you finished tuning?" Asuka asked, walking over and carrying her own eupho. It gleamed moonlight-silver in her arms. Gold and silver. They were the same instrument, but with a simple change in color, they impressions they gave off differed quite a bit.

"Ah, not yet."

"Oh? Well, you better be quick about it."

"Okay!"

Kumiko blew several long tones, tuning it to compensate for its warmth. All the while, Asuka stood next to her, waiting for her to finish.

"Asuka, are you nervous?" Kumiko asked, putting her tuner in her pocket.

Asuka shifted her instrument in her arms and stuck her tongue out a bit bashfully. "Just a little."

"I've been a wreck since yesterday. Midori's fine, though."

"She's amazing, that girl." Asuka laughed, and Kumiko nodded her agreement. "...It's kinda sad, though."

"What is?"

"This has been so much fun, but it's gonna be over soon. I don't want the performance to be over. I just want summer to keep going," Asuka said, then smiled a self-reproachful little smile. Her long eyelashes lowered. With her eyes downcast like that she looked terribly grown-up, and seeing this Kumiko couldn't help but feel a certain forlornness.

She shook her head to throw the feeling off. "What are you talking about, Asuka?"

"Hm?"

"Today isn't our last performance. We're going to Nationals, after all."

Asuka's eyes showed alarm at Kumiko's statement, and then she exploded with laughter. Her delicate, pale fingers lightly patted Kumiko's shoulder. "...Hah, that's right, we said we were gonna go to Nationals."

"That's right!"

"Heh. Well, let's both do our best," said Asuka with a wave.

Her pale hand seemed to melt into her euphonium's silver surface, as though the two were one.

As the moment of their performance approached, Kumiko moved with the band to a small hall for their final sound check. The competition had already started in the main hall, and a special room had been prepared where bands could play without disturbing the performance. This rehearsal hall was near the main hall, and it was functionally the last place where the students would be able to make sure they were ready to play.

"Everyone! Gather round!" Taki clapped his hands. Instead of his normal clothing, he was smartly dressed in a black suit. It made him look extremely gallant and stylish, and girls from other schools who passed him in the halls had squealed when they'd seen him.

"We don't have much time until we go on, so I'd like to check the first opening."

"Yes, sir!"

After they had played the opening phrases of both the compulsory and free pieces several times, Kitauji High School's practice time came to an end.

The most terrifying aspect of playing a brass instrument was making a mistake with the very first sound. The higher the note, the higher that risk was. And once you stumbled over the first note, it was difficult to recover. Kumiko supposed this was why Taki had wanted to make doubly certain of each piece's opening.

"If you play with the same energy you use during practice, each note will naturally lead to the next. Don't think you need to play with more energy or power than you usually do. Let's play the way we always do, and go home smiling."

"Yes, sir!"

The students' faces were bold and resolute. Taki regarded them, satisfied, then slowly smiled.

"Well, then, Miss Ogasawara. Please give us some final words as our band president."

"Huh? Me?!" the suddenly called-upon president cried out. She looked to Asuka for salvation, but Asuka seemed entirely disinclined to answer any such pleas, instead flashing a thumbs-up. *Good luck!* was all she was going to offer, apparently.

"Well, um," Ogasawara stumbled over her words, obviously flustered as her gaze flicked to and fro. Finally she seemed to find some resolve; her hands balled up into fists. "I-I think everybody's worked really hard to get this far. Now all we have to do is bring that hard work together for ten more minutes. So…let's have a cheer for Kitauji!"

She then paused for a deep, lung-filling breath.

"Kitauji, *fight!*"

"*Yeah!*"

The band responded in unison, the sound echoing in the hall. The energy made the air tremble.

"Kitauji High School—It's time."

A woman from the event staff opened the door. Once the door was open, any noise was prohibited. After they ascended the dimly lit stairs before them, they would be at the backstage of the main hall. As the other students milled about around her, Kumiko froze in hesitation. Then—someone tapped her shoulder.

"Let's do this."

The figure who spoke as she passed jauntily by was Reina, holding her trumpet. Despite her impending solo, she seemed utterly calm. Kumiko took a step forward, swearing to herself that this year—*this* year—Reina would have nothing to cry about.

On stage, Rikka High School had already begun their performance. A black curtain blocked the view, but at the corners, the dashing figures of a few Rikka students were slightly visible. Rikka had already moved on to their free performance, which meant that Kitauji would soon be taking the stage. As everyone in the band silently strained to hear Rikka's playing, over on one side Kumiko tried to calm her heart.

The closer the main event drew, the louder its pounding became. It had long since passed the "pitter patter" threshold, and was now much closer to "boom boom." She'd been nervous before competitions in middle school, too, but none of those compared to this. Backstage was dim, but the stage itself was brilliantly lit. Just imagining herself in that light was enough to send her heart racing still faster. An unpleasant sweat oozed from her forehead. She couldn't hear the other school's performance at all. Her hands trembled.

Wait, how does that melody go? How do I move my fingers, again?

Basic questions fell from her brain. A single worry sparked a dozen more. Things she should have memorized, things she should have been able to do without thinking, suddenly they all became impossible. *What am I gonna do? I've forgotten how to play!* Her feverish confusion wiped away all traces of remaining calm. Rikka's performance was nearing its climax. It would be over soon. *What should I do? I can't play! This has never happened before!* Her vision seemed to go dark. A sudden desire to flee the stage seized her. *What should I do? What should I do? What should I do?* Uncertainty ruled her consciousness. The heat of her body was collecting behind her eyes. Kumiko covered her face, hoping that nobody would notice.

"Hey." Suddenly someone tugged on her shirt. Kumiko reflexively turned.

Standing right there was Shuuichi. She got the feeling that it had been quite a while since the two of them had stood face-to-face like this.

He leaned in close to her ear, perhaps out of concern for the backstage rule against talking. When he spoke, it was almost a whisper.

"You okay?"

"I'm fine. No problem." Kumiko quietly shook her head.

Shuuichi frowned sourly. "That's not a 'no problem' face."

"I'm just a little nervous."

"Just a little, huh," said Shuuichi, exhaling an exasperated breath. Despite having avoided her for so long, he was acting very normal. Finding this suspicious, Kumiko silently stepped on his foot.

Ow, he mouthed. "What was that for?"

"Nothing."

"Jerk." Shuuichi slumped.

Kumiko caught the traces of a smile at the corners of his mouth but couldn't say anything—because she'd realized what he'd been doing. He roughly patted her back. His fingertips were trembling.

"It'll be fine. Think of all the practice we did."

Despite the encouraging words, his face as he turned his attention back to his own instrument was somehow pathetic. This seemed terribly funny for some reason, and Kumiko felt her nervousness give way and crumble with a *snap*. Warmth returned to her frozen fingers, and her worry-addled brain started working again.

From the other side of the black curtain she could hear thunderous applause. There in the backstage gloom, she saw Shuuichi's expression stiffen. Kumiko held her euphonium close. The golden horn in her arms sparkled even here, where there shouldn't have been any light. It would be okay. She could do this. A strangely warm certainty welled up inside Kumiko. Wanting to share it, she gently brushed Shuuichi's finger.

He drew a sharp breath and turned to look her way, surprised.

Their eyes met. Their touching fingers gradually intertwined. From the places where skin met skin bloomed a comforting warmth.

"—The next performance will be program number thirty-three: Kitauji Prefectural High School."

At the sound of the announcer's voice, the band moved together. Kumiko went to the euphoniums' seats, and Shuuichi to the trombones', each band member proceeding to the place from which they would fulfill their roles. The concert hall's lights dimmed, leaving them surrounded by a dim gloom.

"The performance will be 'East Coast Pictures' by Nigel Hess, with Noboru Taki conducting."

With the announcement, light flooded the stage. Taki bowed his head, and applause seemed to burst from the hall. He rose from his bow, then ascended the conductor's podium. Blazing light overflowed upon the stage. The stage was always thus—too bright to see anything else. The audience, the judges. Everything unnecessary was brushed aside, leaving behind only the music.

There was a pregnant silence. Murmurs quieted as the audience turned their attention to the stage. This was the entire world, or at least that was how it felt. The baton rose, and the band readied their instruments. The energy in the hall concentrated to a point. Tension burned like fire in Kumiko's throat. The members of the band had given everything in service to the next twelve minutes. Kumiko wanted to win with all her being. The euphonium in her arms twinkled as though it were a living, breathing thing.

And then the baton came down.

The music carrying the dreams of Kitauji High School had only just begun.

♪ Epilogue ♪

Hundreds of gazes focused on the same spot. The atmosphere was tinged with a swirling, feverish energy that brought a flush to the girls' faces. Kumiko slowly exhaled, trying to steel herself against the contagious emotion. Her heartbeat hammered in her eardrums. Her fingernails pressed crescent-shaped marks into the sweat-sticky palms of her clenched fists.

"Eeeek, I'm so excited!" cried Midori childishly next to her. To Midori's other side was Hazuki, who looked about to burst into tears from nerves.

ALL-KYOTO CONCERT BAND COMPETITION, read the simple, vertically lettered sign. Kumiko had seen the characters so many times she was starting to hate them.

"This is it—" came the words from no one in particular. Men carrying a large sheet of paper slowly advanced to the front of the stage. All eyes were upon them. Kumiko felt like her heart was going to leap, flea-like, out of her chest. She was feverish and faint. She pressed her hands hard against her reddening cheeks and watched the paper intently.

The men slowly unrolled the paper, revealing a list of middle schools' names. Next to the names were written the characters for "gold," "silver," and "bronze." Before she could even think of finding her own school's name, something struck Kumiko from behind.

"Kumiko!"

She looked immediately back. Embracing her tightly from behind was Reina, eyes red and shedding great, glittering teardrops.

"Wha—" The moment she saw Reina's expression, Kumiko's heart froze. Had they failed again? Had she let Reina cry again? Kumiko held her breath, unable to put any of this into words. Reina's slender arms wrapped around Kumiko's neck.

"Kansai!"

"Huh?" Kumiko replied in spite of herself at the unexpected word.

Reina forcefully rubbed her eyes and wrapped Kumiko in another tight embrace. "Kansai! We're going to Kansai!"

Her words slowly penetrated Kumiko's ears. It took some time for her brain to process them. Kumiko's eyes slowly widened. Behind her, Hazuki's voice rose in a shrill cry.

"Whoa! Kansai!"

The shouts spread infectiously. Kumiko reflexively looked back to Reina. Reina's cheeks were red, and her usual composure was completely absent.

"I can't believe it! Kansai! *Kansai!* Kumiko!"

"Yeah. It's true."

"I'm so happy I could die! Seriously!" Reina said, a huge, shy smile on her face.

The moment she saw that face, Kumiko felt the strength drain out of her legs. Reina's eyes went saucer-wide. "Whoa—are you okay?"

Her throat was hot. A feeling like being caught in a tight hug lingered there, and she had no words. Reina peered at her, concerned. Kumiko opened her mouth to try to speak, but all that emerged was a whisper of a breath. She felt dizzy. She'd lost all strength in her arms. Kumiko gave up trying to clasp the hands of the girl in front of her. The world blurred. Her eyes filled with something hot.

"...I'm so glad. I'm so, so glad." Kumiko finally managed. She wiped her eyes with her hands, leaving behind glittering droplets on her skin. "Reina, I'm so happy."

Reina nodded hugely. "Me too!" she cried, and caught Kumiko up in another embrace.

The band's happy buzzing did not subside for some time. Apparently unable to bear it any longer, Taki clapped his hands twice. The students all turned toward the director at the sound. Standing next to Taki as usual was Michie, dabbing at the corners of her eyes with a tissue.

Taki looked over the band members and smiled mischievously. "You all seem to think this is the story's happy ending, but practice for the Kansai Regionals begins tomorrow. Our goal is the National Concert Band Competition. Let's all do our very best to make sure that things don't end here," said Taki, his eyes merrily narrow.

Just then, Kumiko realized that those same eyes were wet, too. She felt ticklish, restless. She wanted to play her instrument. The rising desire trembled in her chest.

"Now then, I will see you all tomorrow at nine AM in the music room for practice. We have to win the next one, too!"

Hearing this, Kumiko took a deep breath.

"Yes, sir!"

There under the blue summer sky, the students' voices sounded out, high and strong.